Shiny Objects

The Iowa School of Letters Award for Short Fiction

Prize money for the award is provided by a grant
from the Iowa Arts Council

Shiny Objects

Dianne Benedict

IOWA CITY
UNIVERSITY OF IOWA PRESS

The previously published stories in this collection appear by permission:

"Looking for Rain," *INTRO 10* (Fall 1979).

"Crows," *fiction international* (Fall 1980).

"Shiny Objects," *The Atlantic Monthly* (February 1982).

"Where the Water Is Wide," *The Atlantic Monthly* (May 1982).

LIBRARY OF CONGRESS CATALOGING IN PUBLICATION DATA

Benedict, Dianne, 1941-
  Shiny objects.

  (The Iowa School of Letters award for short fiction)
  Contents: Crows – The blind horse – Shiny objects
– [etc.]
  I. Title.   II. Series.
PS3552.E539585 1982   813'.54   82-10853
ISBN 0-87745-116-8
ISBN 0-87745-117-6 (pbk.)

University of Iowa Press, Iowa City 52242

FOR LADY
who showed me the small path

Contents

Crows

Evening was spreading over the long sweep of the land, darkening the prickly-pear cactus into soft, hulking shapes that appeared to be folding slowly towards the ground, like sheep for the night. A man was traveling along the shoulder of the road. He was a tall, gaunt man with a head that jutted forward, and he carried a shotgun swinging easily in one hand. He moved lightly, almost but not quite running. He wore an olive-green jacket and a felt hat, both greased with sweat, and a pair of heavy wool pants that lacked a number of inches in meeting up with his shoes.

Suddenly all the long, careless bones of this man drew together, as if someone had tugged on a string at the center of him, and in the space of a few seconds he had melted soundlessly into the ditch at his side, raised his gun to the bead, and, without pause, pulled the trigger. In the deepening, slow-breathing evening air, the sound of this shot breaking barrier after barrier across the countryside was like the end of the world.

The man darted forward a few paces and froze. Then the string at his center fell slack, and, pushing his hat back on his head, he rose to his full height, and spit sideways at a cedar post. He cracked his gun open and removed the spent shell.

A few yards ahead of him something rustled the weeds in the ditch. A large black fan spread open there, then another, and the thing bumped forward, scrabbling along the rocky ground, and then sank on its side.

The man cradled the gun in his arm, went forward and stood looking down at the thing in the weeds.

"Half shot you a crow, have you, Myron?" he said. "Well, shit!"

The old clay-colored truck barrelled noisily through the growing darkness. Beneath the clatter of the stones in the truckbed, the tires hummed monotonously on the concrete road, and the tinny music from the radio drifted in snatches over the darkening range like reflections from a brightly colored Chinese lantern over a vast black lake.

Everything inside the cab was bathed by the green-white light from the dash. A small, plastic dancer in a real grass skirt was secured by a suction cup to the shelf behind the seat, and a pair of giant foam-rubber dice hung from the rear-view mirror.

The old concrete road that the truck was moving on passed eventually in front of a nightspot called The Abandoned Hope. This was a place near the reservoir, with live music and a few cabins around it, and was very popular with the colored folk.

Next door to The Abandoned Hope was a small, run-down establishment for buying and selling used cars. It was owned by a man named Rich Stutts, a wiry, short-legged individual who dressed, winter and summer, in army fatigues with the sleeves ripped off the shirt. When the clay-colored truck was still about ten miles down the road, Stutts was standing in front of a fragment of mirror that he had propped up in his kitchen, combing his carrot-colored hair forward into a shelf over his eyes. Before long he and a new girl he had arranged to have for the evening and the two people in the truck would all join up together.

The young man in the truck, whose name was Jim Wesley White, drove with his arm resting on the open window. He steered with one thumb pressed against the bottom of the steering wheel. He wore a dark maroon shirt with a white stripe in it and clean khaki pants, and his straight brown hair, freshly wetted and parted in the middle, still showed the marks of the comb. He was twenty-one years old. He smelled of starching and ironing and Old Spice cologne, and he had a look of mystical innocence in his dark blue eyes.

2

Every few minutes he glanced at his companion. This was a young woman with heavy, dark-brown hair held back by two tortoise-shell combs. She wore a flower-print dress with white cuffs and collar, and she had a handkerchief with pansies on it tucked in her belt. She sat with her hands in her lap, mile after mile, looking out the open window.

After they had gone a long while without conversation, Jim Wesley made a small adjustment to the rear-view mirror. "Have you ever been out to the lake?" he said.

"Yes," she said.

He looked carefully into the mirror from several angles. "Do you know a man out there name of Stutts?" he said.

"Yes."

"That's where I work. I work at his place," he said.

"What do you do there?"

"Fix cars," he said.

"He has owned that place a long time," she said.

"Yes," he said. "He says he knows you."

She turned and looked at him for the first time since they had left the city. "What did he say about me?" she asked.

"Oh, I don't know. I guess he said something about how you played the organ in church. I said I knew that, naturally."

"I didn't belong to the church when I knew him," she said.

"Oh," he said. "Well, I guess he knew of it somehow."

Again, they drove in silence. Jim Wesley thought about the time, a little more than a week ago, when he and Stutts were sitting on the old split-up car seat in front of the shop eating freeze-dried salted corn out of the little packages that were sold in the vendor.

"I knew her ten years ago when she was maybe sixteen years old," Stutts had said, and then he had had a great deal to tell about her, most of which was impossible to believe.

"It's not the same one," Jim Wesley had said.

"It is. I know her. It's her." Stutts patted his pockets and brought out his cigarettes. "She was altogether different then," he said. "It was like some kind of voltage always

3

coming out from her. Wasn't any way to understand her. She just started following me around. Just started coming out here to the lake all by herself in her Daddy's car. By God, I still puzzle over her."

"The way I heard it, she won't go out with anybody," Jim Wesley said.

Stutts laughed at him and flicked a kernel of corn at him that struck him on the forehead. "Maybe she would with a virgin," he said.

Jim Wesley reached over and emptied one of the bags of corn into Stutt's breast pocket and then laid his hand on the bulge. "Miss Eugenia," he said, "Would it make any difference if I told you I was a virgin?"

"Darling boy, it surely would," said Stutts. "I have to confess a weakness for virgin boys."

"Well, here I am," Jim Wesley said, and he grabbed Stutts by the head, and Stutts shoved him hard so that he fell off the seat onto the ground. He had wrapped his arms around Stutts' legs then, and Stutts had fought him off and kicked dirt on him and had gone, laughing, back into the shop.

Now, riding in the truck, he stole glances at her. She was quiet, strong-looking. Her arms were smooth and white, and the curve of her throat moved him, made him feel as if he were sinking, drowning even.

Before the talk with Stutts, he had never thought much of her. When she played the organ in church she had always seemed plain and somewhat awkward, sitting up on a level above the congregation. He had always thought of her, when he thought of her at all, as a sort of handmaiden of the Christ among the lilies that looked down on everyone from the stained-glass window over her head. But after Stutts had spoken with him about her, he had come up and had a conversation with her on the lawn in front of the church. She had said to him in her slow voice, as though it didn't even take any thinking over, that yes she would go with him to the lake, come Saturday night, or wherever he wanted to go.

Her father, a large man with pale, shaking hands, had been sitting on the porch swing when Jim Wesley drove up to the house. The father was drinking wine from a plastic glass, and the bottle was on the floor under the swing. The man's handshake was moist and needful. His eyes begged for something. He had been a widower for years. Eugenia had stood at the edge of the porch steps, looking out over the yard while Jim Wesley extricated himself.

Now, riding next to her in the truck, he thought about what Stutts had told him about the way she had been. She had got religion, evidently. He pictured pulling the combs from her hair on each side, watching it fall forward.

Her hands with their long, smooth fingers rested in her lap, the palm of one turned upward. It was still with him, from when she got into the car, the way her legs had swung in together, long and strong under the thin, flowered cloth.

She would at least go walking with him by the lake, he thought. Stutts would have the cabin ready like they had planned, but they wouldn't necessarily have to use it. He didn't know if they would use it. Sometimes, when he looked at her, he wanted to go into the cabin with her like he had thought about; but at other times, especially when he looked over at her hands, at the one so relaxed with the palm turned upward, he would feel a dull cold in his legs and belly, and then it seemed to him that all that business related to the cabin was impossible even to consider.

She couldn't say why she had come with him. Remembering back, she thought perhaps she had come with him because the smell of his after-shave lotion reminded her of being in school, and she had momentarily slipped back to that time when, whatever a boy asked you, you said yes.

Then she remembered distinctly that the moment he'd asked her to come with him she'd had a sudden vision of the house she lived in with her father, and how dark it was in a certain corner where the stair turned, and up a little higher, on the second landing, a small wire cage that had

5

hung there as long as she could remember, with a few hulls still in the feed cup and the little wire door standing open.

When he had asked her out, she had been excited to picture sitting on the steps of the porch for the next few evenings thinking about going. Even though he was too young for her. She had felt a little pull, like the tension of a spring, under her breastbone.

She had been aware of him a long time at church. She had been very drawn to him for about a year now, maybe, and it had made her happy to have this feeling for him secretly without him knowing. She was struck by how perfectly proportioned everything was about him—the shape of his head, his brown hands that she could tell were not hard like a man's usually were, his eyes under the straight brows looking as though nothing could ever damage him, or even touch him, like stars glimpsed remotely through a tear in the clouds.

She wasn't able to look at him while they drove. She watched, in a long sweep of sky, the gold that the sun had left deepen into red. On the radio, a man was singing about how loving a woman was like being taken by the ocean farther and farther from shore.

"Look up ahead," Jim Wesley said. He was leaning forward peering through the windshield. The truck slowed.

"It's Myron Bless," he said.

"Who is that?" she said, but her voice was covered by the whine of the gears as they pulled off the road.

They drew up alongside a man in a felt hat and a jacket that was out at the elbows. The man squinted against the headlights and then stepped closer to the truck and bent down to look inside. He had a cracked-open gun slung over one arm, and with his other hand he held a crow by its thick black feet.

"Hey there, Myron," said Jim Wesley. "What are you doing out here?"

"Guess I'm after crow," the man said. He had a voice like a nail coming out of the wood slowly. "Or else they're after me."

Eugenia, watching the crow's head, saw a topaz eye appear, and then the man stepped back and smacked the head against a cedar post. After that he gave the crow a hard little shake as if he expected something to fall out of it, and the beak and eye widened simultaneously and there was a great swelling of feathers ending in a shudder.

"I wouldn't keep on with that business," Eugenia said, but then the man was coming towards them and looking inside again.

"I'm about ready to fold it up," he said. "You going to the lake, I'd appreciate the ride."

"Climb in," said Jim Wesley. He was already shifting gears. The man tossed the crow carelessly into the ditch behind him and went thumping up into the truck bed, and then they were once more on the road.

"Isn't much to look at, is he?" said Jim Wesley.

"Who is he?" she said.

"Myron Bless. Works for Stutts," he said.

She turned around and looked through the dusty back window at the felt hat that rubbed against the glass.

"What does he do?" she asked. She remembered the defiant topaz eye, the clenched black feet.

"Whatever he's told," he said.

Stutts took the girl by the wrist and pressed her hand up into the small of her back. He steered her through all the slow-moving black people on the dance floor. He found a little space for them to move around in, and he put his hands on her hips as she began to pick up the beat of the music. She was a new girl, a real dresser. She had on a tight-fitting silver dress with a halter top, and a cluster of rhinestones on a black ribbon around her neck. She had arranged her red hair into a twist on top of her head, and under the blunt-cut bangs her eyelids glistened with green and silver dust.

When the musicians stopped for a break, Stutts took the girl over to the bar. After he had ordered the drinks, he put his hand on her back and massaged her neck a little, and she smiled and gave him a long look that said, yes, she was feeling that way, too. He offered her a cigarette and she took it and ran it slowly through her fingers while he lit the match.

The bartender brought the drinks and wiped the beads of water off the bar with his apron. "Jim Wesley White was looking for you a while back," he said.

Stutts swung around on the stool and looked out over the barroom, which was so dark and crowded it was hard to recognize anyone, but then he saw Jim Wesley and Eugenia sitting together at a table by the door.

The girl in the silver dress leaned close and said, "Who's looking for you?" and he squeezed her arm, high up where he could feel the warmth of her underarm, and then he left the bar and made his way across the room towards the other two.

When he leaned down between them and said, "I can get you a better table," Eugenia drew back as if there had been a bright light turned on her and looked up at him with her face tight as though against the glare of it.

Stutts said, "Miss Crawford and I have met before, or do I disremember," and she said, "No, that's right."

White smiled back and forth at the two of them and said, "What do you know about that."

Then the girl from the bar came up and asked to be introduced.

It was well into the evening when Stutts asked Eugenia to dance. He picked a slow number and pulled her to him as soon as they reached the floor. She moved lightly against him, not holding onto him noticeably, but not pulling away, either.

"Been a long time, isn't it?" he said, and she said, "Since what?"

"Since we were dancing together," he said.

She made no reply.

"Hell, since we got this close or anything," he said.

"It was nine years ago," she said.

"I always did remember you," he said. He drew back and looked down at her. She was looking away to the side.

"I knew you only about a month in the summer, I think maybe it was ten years ago," she said.

"But you never did forget me, neither."

"That's right," she said.

He smiled down at her. "You remember all that?" he asked her.

She looked up at him with that look like being under too bright a light again, and said, "Do I remember all what?"

"You and me," he said.

"And the others?" she said.

He thought she meant maybe some other girls who must have been in the picture at the time, but she said, "I mean those others you liked to bring along," and then he remembered. He remembered a night when he had taken her out to the other side of the lake, and they had picked up two of his buddies on the way. He remembered getting her to lie with him in the back seat. The other men had sat up front, he recalled, drinking their beer slowly and acting like they weren't watching, only they were watching. He recalled how she had lain with him, not pitching in so as you would notice, but not pulling away either.

"I never did understand about that," he said.

She stopped dancing and stood back from him and looked up at him with an expression he couldn't put a name to.

"I mean that whole business there at the end," he said. "That's what we're talking about, isn't it?"

"It was a long time ago," she said.

"Well, sure," he said.

"But I still remember it," she said.

He stared at her. She had taken a handkerchief from her belt and was pressing it where the sweat glinted on her upper lip and under her eyes. A large man behind her bumped against her shoulder and she dropped the handkerchief, but she was walking away by then and she didn't stop to pick it up.

Eugenia walked with Jim Wesley on a path crossed with

roots under some live oak trees on their way to the cabins. The cabins were duplexes, sided with brown asbestos shingles. They stood in a row, with carports between them. Beside each door grew a young cedar tree about the size of a ten-year-old child.

"We can probably sleep in the truck if you're worried about how it looks," Jim Wesley said.

"There's nobody looking at us," said Eugenia.

"Or I could maybe go leap off the pier," he said laughing, "and if I didn't drown I'd probably come up sober." He could barely walk. She had to keep her arm around him.

They reached the step of their cabin, and she took the key from him and opened the door.

"We're lucky to have a place," she said.

"Hell, yes, we have a place," he said. He held onto the doorsill and put his other arm around her shoulders. "Stutts would have given us *any* place. Hell, we could have had *his* place."

"He had this place ready all along," she said.

"Oh, I don't know if you can go so far as to say that," he said.

"You are too drunk to lie," she said. She put an arm around his waist and helped him through the door. He stood there looking around as though he'd never seen a bedroom before in his life.

The walls of the room were covered with a dull brown wallpaper that had strips of some kind of flowers in it. A merciless glare fell sharply on everything from a small ceiling fixture with brass arms and four glass tulips. There was a spindly iron bed covered with a quilt, and a dresser with a round mirror in a frame of heavy roses. Thrown down on the cracked linoleum, with its border of ivy vine, were a half dozen rag rugs.

Eugenia led Jim Wesley to the bed. He fell upon it and immediately lay still and went to sleep. She sat beside him, looking for a long time at the dark window where she saw herself reflected. Then she slipped his shoes off his feet, placed them under the bed, and went into the bathroom.

While she was there she was sure she smelled the smoke from Stutts' cigarettes. He'd been in there, alright, she thought. He'd been in there, picturing how it would be. Well, he could never have in mind the way a thing really was. He could never have any part of it. He would always be thinking one thing, and the way it really was would be another. What did she care what he thought he had? She could let him have it, it was no part of her.

She was washing her face when she saw the two rubbers on a shelf over the sink. She stood with the water dripping from her face, thinking, of course, one for tonight, and one for in the morning. She picked one up and slipped it out of its little paper band and looked closely at it. Then she put the paper band back on it and laid the rubber on the shelf exactly where it had been. It was nothing to her.

She came out of the bathroom and walked barefoot over to the door to switch off the light. She took off her dress and slip in the moonlight and hung them in the closet, and then she took off her brassiere and folded it and put it in the single drawer of the stand beside the bed.

She started to undo Jim Wesley's pants, but he came alive suddenly, distressed and feverish-looking. "It was those damn mice got under the clutch plate," he said. He pushed her roughly away and got up and stepped out of his pants. Then he got back in bed, under the covers. She watched the pinched look ease from around his eyes, and then he was asleep again.

She got in beside him and looked for a long time at his face. There were pale, milky shadows moving over him. The moon was bright in the room, and, in the brightness outside, she could see heavy rocking shadows cast down by the live oak trees.

She lifted back the quilt and then the sheet. He lay on his side with his legs drawn up. His hands were pressed together between his thighs. She opened his shirt and folded it back and laid her hand on his chest. She put her mouth where his neck curved into his shoulder and moved closer to him and pressed her breasts against him. She slipped

11

her hand down over his ribs and round over the curve of his back and after that she took a long time feeling him everywhere, slowly, because there was no reason not to in the quiet room, no reason at all.

Sometime later, in the room on the other side of the wall, Myron Bless eased himself down into a wicker chair. He had a package of cigarettes in his pocket that he'd taken off of Stutts. When he took the package out, he found that he was down to the last cigarette. When he took that one out he flattened the package and made a hard twist out of it and dropped it on the floor.

It was dark in the room. Every now and then the blind would billow out at the window and then rest back with a little tapping sound. Myron pinched the last inch of the cigarette between his forefinger and thumb, and each time he took a draw he held it up and watched the ember.

He was thinking about his first time and the boy it had been with. He hadn't thought on all that in a long time. He eased back into his memory gingerly, feeling all along if it was wise, and he knew, remembering, that that first one was the only one worth thinking back on. He had always known that. Long, boney, waterfront trash that boy had been, that first one, name of Kelly from a family of brothers that worked a trawler. Was no place to meet with him except under the wharf. They hadn't known the first thing about it, hadn't even known enough to bring something to put under them. It had only been just feeling each other, showing each other a little at a time, until the boy had told him one night that some other boy had showed him the way. Behind the unblinking ember, Myron laughed low in his throat. That's what the boy had called it, "the way," as if there was only that one. This is the way, the boy would say, and there in the dark wedge under the wharf, with chinks of light sliding over them as they moved, and now and then a heavy tread on the boards above them from some bloke come out to piss – there they would have what they wanted, and it was all there with that boy, by God, more than it had ever been again. He watched the tiny glow-worms winding on the ember of the cigarette. You spend a lifetime looking, he thought, and all along it was only just that once, but you could never guess it. Not until it was all played out from here to hell and back, and it had let go of you, finally, and you didn't care no more. It was all only brackish water save for a time going too fast under a wharf, the deep sun-red of the arms starting at the shoulders and then the long white length of that boy, all hipbones and the hollows in the flanks, all that warm slippery business.

He felt for the ashtray on the stand beside the chair and ground out the cigarette.

Stutts would have that new girl with him, so there was no going home. Maybe he would walk by the lake until the first light, or maybe he would bed down in the boathouse. It was the sound of the water under the wharf made that a good place. Stutts would sleep late with the girl. Time to check in on them would be around ten, maybe eleven. Be about then they'd be ready for breakfast. Maybe today they would go on the shoot. It had been the crow he had got by mistake had put him in mind of it, and he had brought up the idea when Stutts had come home with the girl, and Stutts had said, hell, why not, if he was back up on his feet by then.

Myron opened the door without touching the knob and eased the screen-door open and stepped out onto the porch. He looked down the long, shadow-banded path towards the lake. He felt the moonlight on his face and shoulders, blue and bright and quiet. He patted his pocket for the cigarettes, then remembered they were gone. After a moment he stepped down onto the path.

Eugenia knew there was someone in the other room. There had been no sound, but the smell of smoke had come again strongly, and she knew with some slow-rising sense that there was someone there, and then she heard a small sound on the path and knew that he had gone.

She got up and took her watch out of the pocket of her dress and looked at it, and then she went and stood in front of a picture hanging on the wall between the two rooms. It was a picture of three cowboys around a fire, with a horse tied up in the background. One man was playing the harmonica and the two others were smiling at each other across the fire. One of the smiling men was bent forward passing a plate with a fish on it across to the other one.

Eugenia went up and took the picture down and stood looking at a hole in the wall. She put her hand in the hole and felt wood at the back of it. Then she found the place on the picture where there was a slit in the paper just wide enough to look through. She put the picture down and went out onto the porch.

The door to the other room was ajar, and when she went in, the smell of smoke was strong and also the feeling was very strong that the person had just left.

She switched on the lights. On the floor, propped up against the wall between the two rooms, was a picture of a Japanese woman holding a small brown bird on the back of her hand. On the wall above the picture there was a length of wood that could be pushed aside. When Eugenia pushed it aside and looked through, she saw Jim Wesley asleep in the moonlight, uncovered except for one leg wrapped in the sheet.

She turned and looked about the room. The bed looked as though it was made up with only the spread, without any sheets or blankets underneath. There were cigarette butts in an ashtray beside the chair. She bent to pick up a twisted cigarette package that lay on the floor, knowing it was a package of Stutts' Lucky Strikes even before she spread it open.

"He was watching us," she said.

She moved in front of the long mirror over the dresser. Slowly she raised her arms with the wrists crossed and

14

looked at herself that way. She was the color of plaster in the harsh light. Her dark nipples were stark on her white body and her shoulders were nothing but bone. Her eyes were like live coals far back in a cave.

She leaned over and pushed an ashtray across the glass top of the dresser slowly until it reached the edge and dropped off. There was a vase on the dresser also, half full of water but without any flowers in it, and she pushed that slowly over the edge, too.

Then she crossed the room and sat on the edge of the bed. She sat there looking down at her hands pressed together between her knees. After a while she lay back. She lay stretched out on the bed for a long time, with her eyes open, under the harsh overhead light. It was like being under the eye of the sun in the desert. Some time later, when the dawn came, she was still lying there in the same position, but her eyes were closed by then and she was asleep.

Later that day Jim Wesley sat beside Eugenia in the back of the truck taking a hard ride. Stutts was up front, driving, with the girl from the night before beside him, and also Myron Bless. They drove over rough terrain, swerving constantly to avoid the pricklebush and low mesquite, heading out for a place Myron knew about that he said was virgin ground.

Jim Wesley would have had no wish to speak, even if he could have been heard over the crack of stones on metal. He rode along with his eyes fixed on the guns. There were five guns—the three shotguns, and the two rifles for the women. Packed alongside of them was a wooden toolbox, a cooler full of drinks, and a small battery-operated gramaphone that Stutts had wrapped up in a blanket.

It was a long ride. It seemed to Jim Wesley like it would go on forever. They had been driving across open country for an hour, and now it was well on towards evening, with the sun sinking low enough to be flattening out, and the beginning of a thin pollen-colored haze drifting up from the horizon.

15

After a while the truck lurched and slowed down as Stutts shifted gears; then they took a sudden turn and picked up speed again. Jim Wesley hauled himself up, bracing against the wind, and saw that they were approaching three great wide-spreading live oak trees, darkly silhouetted, behind which the sun was going down very deep-colored and swollen.

When they were about a quarter mile from these trees, they came to a table of stones that fell away to the trees and beyond them, and Stutts stopped the truck at the edge of this rubble and got out and came around to open the back end. Then Myron got out and came around, too, and they hauled out the toolbox and three of the guns and the blanket with the gramaphone wrapped up in it, and headed for the trees.

Jim Wesley stood in the truck watching as they made their way over the stones. Behind him, Eugenia sat turned in on herself, with her arms around her knees. She was dressed in a long-tailed khaki shirt and a pair of army pants of Stutts'. There was no sound except a slow, melancholy country beat coming from a radio inside the truck.

After a few moments the door of the cab opened slowly and Stutts' girl climbed down, her skirt stretching taut over her thighs. She had on the same spike-heeled shoes and silver dress she'd worn the night before, and a small radio hardly bigger than a package of cigarettes hung from a strap on her wrist. Without closing the door of the truck, she began to make her way unsteadily over the stones, following the men.

"Time to decide," Jim Wesley said.

The music drifted back to them from the girl's radio.

"You going to come?" he said.

Eugenia didn't answer.

"Whatever happened last night, I'm sorry," he said, and, when still she wouldn't answer, he said loudly, "only I swear to God if it's anything like I think it is I only wish I could remember it!"

16

"What do you wish it was?" she said.

"I wish it was just what you think."

"Well," she said, "Then that's what it was."

He thought for a moment. "I don't know that for sure," he said.

She rolled up the cuffs of the army pants. "I'm tired of the whole business," she said. She crawled to the end of the truck and dropped to the ground. He followed her and dropped down beside her and took hold of her arm. Her face turned hard and she tore her arm away from him and started after the others.

He hauled out the cooler with the drinks in it and the two remaining guns and hurried to catch up with her. The day was growing unbearably thin for him, yet still he was caught up in an expectation that was without name or reason, and he rushed foolishly after her, stumbling over the stones, with the two guns clutched awkwardly against him, and the cooler getting tangled up with his legs.

When he was even with her, she stopped and put her hands in her pockets and turned halfway towards him. "You were asleep," she said.

"When?" he said.

She lifted the edge of a stone with her foot, turned it over carefully. "You don't even have any idea of it. About all that," she said.

"About all what?" he said, and she glanced at him, frowning, with her face tight against him and then she turned and walked away.

"Listen," he said.

"I'm tired of the whole business," she said.

"Now, wait a minute," he said, and he began to hurry after her again, but then he stumbled over the cooler and had to set it down, hard, on the ground in front of him. "What the hell's the sense in keeping secrets?" he called, but she had gotten far away by then and had no interest in even turning around to look at him, and so he didn't care to call out to her any longer.

"Bitch," he said softly.

He left the cooler sitting where it was. He went on towards the group of people under the trees. Someone else was going to have to come back for the cooler. It wasn't going to be him. The sun, setting behind the trees, cast long shadows towards him. He stopped and looked back at the truck. The door on the passenger side was still open. The truck looked like it was waiting for him. It was his truck. He didn't like it the way Stutts had driven it over the rough terrain. He was always careful about his truck, treating it as if it had feelings, and it had lasted him a long time. Stutts could ruin a truck in a day. But it was no matter to him, he could always get another one, easy.

Jim Wesley turned and continued, entering the shadow of the trees. No one in the group looked at him. Eugenia was backed up against the trunk, with her shoe off, searching around inside of it for a stone. Myron had his knife out, scraping away at what looked like a three-inch section of bamboo. Stutts lay stretched out on the blanket.

The girl in the silver dress sat off to one side. She was turning the dial on her radio slowly from station to station, searching for something. Snatches of voices slipped out, now a woman, now a man, now a line from a song, broken off.

The first crow appeared out of nowhere. No one saw it come, but suddenly it was there, moving along one of the high-up branches. Myron pointed it out to the others. "Here they come," he said.

Then there was another one, and they all saw that one, and the girl in the silver dress got really excited to shoot at it, but Myron said, "Chrissake, hold onto her, Stutts!" Just then, Jim Wesley called out, "Throw me one of those callers!" and Myron threw him one of the callers he had carved out, and then Myron and Jim Wesley began sending out calls that sounded like crows in a terrible rage.

"By God, they're coming!" said Stutts, and he put a record

on the little gramaphone he'd brought out there. When the record had picked up speed, he set the needle on it and turned the volume up on a recording of about a thousand crows all calling at once. This sound lifted and filled the space, and Myron and Jim Wesley blew more loudly on the callers, getting really excited over the sound of all the crows on the record.

Then there came the first answer from far away in the dark curtain of dust that the wind had blown up off the countryside. It sounded like maybe a half-dozen crows answering from different locations. But then it was as if a tidal wave of crows burst through some smothering barrier with a sound that intensified swiftly until it drowned out the record, and crows began dropping down out of the darkening sky into the trees. In a few seconds, the upper branches were thick with crows, all of them calling, and hundreds more dropping and swooping, until the sky was completely blacked out, and then the men took up the guns and began to shoot.

The crows fell heavily, like stones, and lay on the ground flappling and scrabbling, but still they came as if there was no end of them, flying lower, more brazen, many of them right into the guns. There was no time to count or even take satisfaction in the dead. There was only the rustling mass descending, ever-replenishing, deafening them, and the men loading up and drawing a bead, and blasting off, and doing this over and over, and all the while there were the ones in great number who were moving over the branches, calling and flapping as if there was nothing any different from every other day of their lives.

Then, over the terrible noise of the crows and the guns there came another sound, which was the girl in the silver dress screaming and screaming. Jim Wesley, when finally he heard this, looked over his shoulder and saw the girl with her hands to her face yelling towards Eugenia who lay close-by on the ground with a dark stain spreading beneath her. He gazed without comprehension at this scene and lowered his gun, sensing in that moment that he was the only one shooting. Myron held his gun with the barrel pointed down, and was shaking and white in the face. Stutts had dropped his gun and was waving his hands as if to make everything quiet, and was approaching with careful steps the place where Eugenia lay looking so strange.

The crows overhead went on calling, but the record had played out, and it was quieter, now, after the guns. No one spoke and the girl had stopped screaming.

Stutts went down beside the figure on the ground and bent close over it, but at first didn't touch it.

"She had the gun on you, Stutts," Myron said.

"She had what?" said Jim Wesley.

"I didn't have no other choice, she had the gun on you," Myron said, this time louder, and then he dropped his gun and sat down on the ground with a low cry.

Half an hour later Jim Wesley sat in the back of the fast-moving truck, along with the gear, which had been thrown in helter-skelter. The guns were vibrating and traveling over the truck-bed, first this way and then that. When one of them got too close to him, he would reach for it and throw it over the side of the truck.

The record player still had the little record on it, and the arm with its needle kept bouncing back and forth across it.

He held the body where they had placed it across his knees, wrapped up in the blanket. Again and again (it seemed to him he'd been doing this for days) he had to keep covering it up. Still, she kept getting exposed.

"We'll be there in a minute," he said repeatedly.

He gazed steadily at a streak of red trapped between two blacknesses along the horizon. Above that began the wide expanse of the night, with already a few stars.

20

The Blind Horse

The girl stood beside the road studying the spiky shadow thrown down by a single flowering yucca growing by the barbed-wire fence. Next to the yucca, a red-wing blackbird clung to the top of a post, calling a four-note song again and again into the deepening light of the evening, his glossy tail blown sideways in the wind.

The girl was thin-boned and visibly pregnant. Her short, straight hair was flattened on one side by the wind. She had a wide face, as void of expression as a sheep's, and her flat, deep-blue eyes, behind thick-lensed glasses, were full of an intense, innocent light.

She wore baggy white trousers, with blue rubber sandals, and an olive-green army jacket buttoned tightly over her large middle. A tapestry-cloth bag with bamboo handles rested on the ground at her feet.

Immediately beyond the fence, on both sides of the road, began the vast tracts of cactus and ochre-brown grasses, which had baked under a drought for the whole of the summer. Now, in November, the first cold winds lifted wide drifts of dust off the hard shale. The setting sun was a crimson yoke burning through a haze of this dust. Overhead, the evening sky had taken on an ancient light, as if the Egyptians or the Chaldeans were closing their shades and pulling in the oars of their long boats, and across this illumination, hundreds of calling geese moved in shifting lines from horizon to horizon.

The wind rose again and shook the grasses first on one side of the road and then the other. A slight movement caught the girl's eye, and she looked closely at the ground nearby and made out a brown, horned lizard nearly invisible in the gravel. The lizard raised itself slightly, staring back at her. In that instant she became aware of the sound of a

21

car. Soon, a liver-colored Studebaker with an exposed motor appeared on the road.

The car passed in front of her, slid to a stop, then backed up slowly. Inside was an elderly colored man in a khaki shirt and a battered felt hat very stained about the ribbon. He wore a black string tie held on with a nugget of turquoise. He halted the car and leaned across the front seat.

"Where are you headed, little lady?"

The girl bent down and peered into the car. The skin over the old man's cheeks had a rubbed glow on it, like a horse chestnut, and his eyes were large and womanish.

"That's my business, ain't it?" the girl said.

"You walking?"

"What does it look like?"

"Where you walking from?"

The girl paused. "I don't know," she said. "Town back that-a-way. I cain't remember what they called it."

"You're from the city, aren't you?"

"Maybe."

"Well, you have come a long way out into the wilderness," the old man said, "and it's coming on nightfall."

"No kidding," the girl said.

"Would you like me to take you some place?"

The girl looked down the crumbling concrete road. It swerved neither left nor right, but simply disappeared at a faraway point, flat and empty, into the gathering dusk.

"Maybe," she said.

"You want me to take you back home?"

"Yes," the girl said, glancing again at the lizard, which had reared back farther, exposing a wide, flat belly that looked like the palm of a hand.

"Well, come on and get in, then."

The old man picked up a shovel off the front seat and threw it into the back and swung the car door open. The girl got in, wedging the tapestry-cloth bag under the dashboard.

"Now, whereabouts in the city do you live?" the old man said.

The girl glanced at him quickly and pushed her short hair behind her ears. "Now ain't that something," she said. "I thought you meant *your* home."

"Lord God!" the old man said.

"Listen," the girl said. "Maybe I could just stop over like for one night maybe, you know?"

"Child, I am not equipped," the old man said.

The girl took off her thick-lensed glasses and polished them on the fabric of her jacket. She put them back on and looked at the old man without expression. "Who cares, anyway?" she said. "But it'll cost you five dollars to get me out of the car."

The old man ran his fingers lightly along the bottom of the steering wheel. After a minute, he put the Studebaker in gear and started off. The old car rattled noisily over the tarred cracks in the road, and soon the gearshift began to vibrate. The old man rested his hand on it and drove for a few miles deep in thought. Then he took off his hat and laid it on the seat beside him and ran his hand carefully over his finely moulded, nearly bald head.

"One thing you should know is that I live alone," he said.

"Well, what do you know about that," the girl said.

"Yes," the old man said. "I am an educated man, but I am an old man, and I live alone."

The girl turned her face to the window and let the cold wind blow through her hair.

"What is your name?" the old man said.

"That ain't none of your business, is it?" the girl said. She leaned back and put her feet up on the tapestry-cloth bag and wrapped her arms around her large belly. She rested her head on the back of the seat and closed her eyes.

The Studebaker slammed over a pothole and the girl sat up and saw, a short distance ahead, silhouetted against the deep gold of the sky, a black horse leaning on a black gate. The old man drove up to the gate and stopped. "This here's the property," he said.

She looked through the windshield at the ripples of heat rising out of the motor, and at the silver bulldog attached to the top of the radiator. She studied the big scab-covered horse — clearly a white horse, now, not black — sagging against the gate with its eyes closed. The old man climbed out and swung the gate wide, and the horse got its feet under it eagerly and circled him with a quick step like a pony.

After they drove in, the horse closed the gate with its shoulder and fell into a heavy trot behind the car. The girl turned and watched it through the rear window. The car stirred up a spiral of dust, and the horse ran in the center of this with its ears laid back and its sides heaving, as if it were being tortured.

After a short drive on the rutted dirt road, they pulled into a barren yard, half of which was taken up by a twisted old live oak tree, with many wide-spreading branches resting heavily on the ground. Sagging in the shadow of this tree was a small weathered house, which had beaten paths running from it over to a trough and a windmill. A porch roof, held up with two-by-fours, showed that the house had once possessed a porch, but now there was only a short log rolled up for a step under the door. In the open doorway stood two young goats, twins in every aspect, who stared out at the Studebaker with exactly the same expression.

The old man drove through a half-dozen fox-red hens, which exploded to both sides of the car, and parked in front of the trough by the windmill. He got out, leaving the car door open, and crossed with no great hurry to the house. When he reached the doorway, he lifted the two kids down into the yard; then, holding onto the doorsill with both hands, he climbed up stiffly and disappeared into the dark interior.

The girl got out of the car and stood beside it. The evening had deepened into long shadows, and the sky, reflected brightly in the trough, was like a vast sheet of gold with legion upon legion of small clouds beaten into it.

The girl heard the crash of something heavy in the house, and a moment later, a nanny with large udders leapt from the doorway. The nanny ran with sure feet up one of the branches of the live oak, followed closely by the kids, and the three of them climbed into the heart of the tree and stood there flicking their tails, piercing the stillness of the evening with their bleating.

A light was raised in the house then, and the old man stepped down out of the doorway. In that moment, the white horse, which had slowed to a walk, made its way into the yard. It moved heavily up under the porch roof and leaned against the front of the house, letting all the air out of its lungs explosively.

The old man crossed, unhurried, to the car and took out the girl's bag.

"Notice how fine the light is out here in the evening," he said, turning to where the sun, muted by a violet haze, was setting without ceremony behind the plain curve of the horizon.

"What else is in there?" the girl said, pointing to the house.

"An old cat with double claws," he said.

"Don't you have a barn?"

"Yonder's the shelter for the animals, should they be of a mind to use it," the old man said, nodding to a three-sided shed behind a stand of cedars.

Then he went on towards the house, shuffling a little, humming softly. The girl, following him with her hands in her pockets, picked her way carefully through the chickens. When they came under the porch roof, the old man reached his hand up to the long face of the horse.

"Once, in N'Orleans, I saw a statue of a blue horse," he said, "that grazed the valleys of the Euphrates way before the time of Moses. A great war horse. The image of my friend here. Same arch to the neck." He ran his hand up under the burr mats in the mane, lifting a cloud of dust. "Haunches like a panther."

The girl took in the knobbed spine and the bellied-out sway of the back. She studied the yellow, scarred knees, and the splayed hooves. Then she looked into the horse's eyes, which were transparent as water, with milky, blue-white centers.

"Jesus," she said, "what's wrong with his eyes?"

25

"Why, he's blind," the old man said. The horse snorted softly and rubbed its face on his chest. "He's just an old blind horse." He let the horse blow its warm breath into his hands, then he went on up inside the house.

The girl held onto the doorsill with both hands and stepped up after him into a room which was lit by a warm light from a lantern and smelled of woodsmoke, and fried meat and cherry tobacco.

The old man placed her bag in the corner, then opened the top of a fat-bellied cookstove. He lay the iron lid back carefully with the prong and began filling the stove with wood.

The girl stood to one side of the door studying the room, which was full of the old man's belongings. The lantern shone from the center of a pine table covered with an orange cloth. Resting beside the lantern, in its circle of yellow light, were a Bible and a small silver harmonica.

She watched the old man take a match from the box and strike it on the side of the cookstove. He lowered it, with a hand that shook slightly, to some papers under the wood.

Much of the floorspace in the room was taken up with bundles of thornbranches bound with string. The girl saw, on a sagging shelf, a collection of old wooden radios and many blue-glass jars filled with beets and green beans. Under this was a heap of old jackets crowded onto a row of pegs. She saw, pulled up close to the stove, an aging elephant-footed sofa with a brown cat asleep on it. In front of this sofa, a cotton rope, strung between two chairs, had socks and gray rags dried stiffly across it.

The old man dropped the lid back onto the stove and took a pipe out of his pocket and a small chamois pouch. He loosened the drawstring on the pouch and took out a pinch of tobacco and packed this into the pipe with his forefinger. He struck another match and lit the pipe and, with the smoke gathering in full clouds around him, stood looking into a small cupboard filled with cans.

"Comes down to pork and beans," he said. He took a can

down off the shelf and pounded a pronged opener into it, then sawed around the top, with the can held close to his chest. He dumped the beans into a dented pan. When he turned to set this on the stove, he caught sight of the girl standing in the doorway.

"I am indeed sorry," he said, taking his pipe out of his mouth, "you must be feeling neglected."

"I get allergic to cats," the girl said.

"What, the General? Why, just put him out. It's warm still. He'll get by."

"You put him out," the girl said.

The old man set the pan on the stove and went and laid his hand on the soft fur of the cat's belly, which was turned upward. The cat was old and scarred. It had a big square head and wide, cushion-like paws with too many toes.

"General, you have taken up residence on this couch for ten years, and now the rent's due," the old man said.

The cat opened its eyes halfway and made a small sound in its throat. The old man laid it backwards in his arms and crossed with it to the door. He set it outside on the step. "Stars coming out already. You go on and roam. Go on now."

He closed the door and took the girl by the elbow and led her over to a chair beside the table.

"Sit down, now," he said. "Rest your hands and face."

He took a large spoon from a nail and, with his back to the girl, began stirring the beans. He reached into a cracked bowl for a pinch of salt.

"How come you to run away?" he said.

"My daddy threw me out," the girl said. She picked up the harmonica from the table and put it in the pocket of her jacket.

"What for?"

"What do you mean 'what for?' There ain't any 'what for.' He just threw me out."

"What does he do, your daddy?"

"Lies in bed all day reading westerns," she said. "And

smoking. Seems like everythin' he touches turns to Viceroy cigarettes." She pulled a small silver flask out of her pocket and uncorked the lid and took a long drink from it.

"And your mama?"

The girl snorted, screwing the lid back on the flask.

"She ain't feeling any pain. She's dead."

"I'm sorry."

"Christ! Who cares, anyway?" the girl said. She put the flask back in her pocket and leafed idly through the Bible, then pushed it away from her. "She was took up-country boarded up in a box, back to where she growed up. You ever heard of that happening?"

"Yes."

"She was buried in a little town in the pine trees near a thousand mile up north. She was always saying to me, 'Margaret, you and me are moving back up there together, just the two of us,' and for a long time I thought we really was going to, but after three, maybe four year I just quit listening to her. Then she died."

The old man tapped the spoon on the rim of the pan and reached for two bowls. He filled the bowls with beans and set them on the table.

"May as well tell you I got a brother," the girl said.

"Yes?"

"Brother by the name of Leroy."

"Tell me about your brother," the old man said.

The girl gave a short, hard laugh. "He's a no-account pimple-faced boy that loves to pee on brick walls and spit a lot, and who you can lay bets is going to live out his entire life in the same black leather jacket."

The old man pulled another chair up to the table. He eased himself down into it stiffly and began eating, blowing on each spoonful.

"I got a boyfriend, too," the girl said. "His name is Montgomery. You want to hear a story about him?"

"If you want to tell it."

"Well, it was a few days ago, see, and we was in this booth in this place we go to—just me and Montgomery and Leroy—

and right away Montgomery, he pulls out a comb and starts combing his hair back sort of slow and lazy, and then he pulls out this silver whistle with a little blue ball inside that he knows I love to play with. He drops it down behind the booth where it cain't never be found again. Then he pulls out his knife and flicks it open and lays it in the middle of the table. 'What's the knife for, Montgomery?' Leroy asks him, looking at me, see, and Montgomery says real slow 'thout even raising his voice, 'Oh, 'at's only a little something I laid out there just to show her I ain't the father.'"

The old man turned in his chair and opened the oven door. He took out a small, hot cornbread and broke it in half.

"What do you think about that story?" the girl said.

"When's your baby due to come?" the old man said, laying part of the cornbread beside her bowl.

"Tonight."

For the first time, the old man gave her a direct look. "Tell the truth now," he said.

The girl studied him with no expression whatever. "I don't care if you don't believe me," she said.

"How old are you?"

"Sixteen."

"Yes, and you haven't got nearly your growth. I look at you and I see a large baby inside a child's body."

"My, my," the girl said. "X-ray vision."

"What about tomorrow morning early you and me take a trip over to the doctor in Twin Rivers."

"I ain't going to any doctor," the girl said. "Shove it. I don't even *want* this baby."

"Who's going to love it, then?" the old man said.

The girl snorted. "Who's going to love *me?* You?" She picked up the box of matches and shook it, then threw it back on the table. "Jesus, this is a stupid conversation."

The old man picked up her spoon and slipped it into her hand. "Eat," he said.

"Everybody acts like I'm *diseased* because I don't want it," the girl said. "Course it's no reflection on them that they don't want it. How about you? Do you want it?"

The old man looked up at her thoughtfully. "I am old. Where would I find the years to offer it?"

The girl shoved her hands into the pockets of her jacket and sat looking at him. "What do you know?" she said. "You do want it, don't you?"

The old man looked down again at his bowl and went on eating.

"That's the stupidest thing I ever heard of," the girl said. "Who'd want to live with you? This place smells like goats. This place smells like a barn."

"Listen," the old man said, pushing his bowl away. "You want the bed tonight? What about if we put the feather bed on it?"

"I wouldn't want no colored person raising my baby," the girl said.

The old man placed both hands flat on the table and rose to his feet. "I need to ask for the return of my harmonica," he said.

"What harmonica?" the girl said.

"Take it out of your pocket," the old man said.

The girl took out the harmonica and turned it over slowly in her hands. "Oh, you mean this harmonica," she said. She dropped it onto the table. "I couldn't blow on it after somebody else, anyway."

The old man picked up the harmonica and crossed to the door and took down a black coat.

"Listen. Wait a minute," the girl said.

"The bed's at the top of the stairs," he said. "Clean sheets in the chifforobe. I'll see you in the morning." He opened the door and went out, closing it quietly behind him.

"I don't want your stinking bed!" the girl shouted. She picked up her bowl of beans and threw it against the door. She sat for a long while on the edge of her chair watching the beans slide down the wood. Then she pulled a deep-seated rocker covered with a red blanket up close to the woodstove. She tugged on the bottom of her jacket, easing the tension of it over her belly, and sat down and began rocking steadily.

"He'll be back," she said.

The room grew very quiet. There was only the sound of the rocker. And now and then the blind horse blowing softly outside the window. And the chunks of wood in the wood-stove falling into embers.

The girl woke in the old man's small bedroom under the eaves. She had gone to sleep crosswise on top of the covers, and now felt stiff and cold. A wedge of moonlight cut a path across the quilt and up the wall, which was covered with a water-stained pattern of lilies of the valley, and there, in an oval mirror, was the moon, itself, surprisingly small, netted in the branches of the big oak.

The girl heard music which she thought at first was the radio, but then realized was the old man playing his harmonica.

She pulled the quilt off the bed and wrapped it around her and went to the top of the stairs. From there she could see a small portion of the room below which was lit with a flickering light. She descended the steep steps carefully, holding onto the bannister, and when she was nearly at the bottom she hunkered down and studied the old man, who sat playing quiet, slow chords on his harmonica in the rocker by the fire. The door to the front yard stood open, and the brown cat lay on the table with its paws folded into its breast, watching the old man through half-closed eyes.

The room, lit by the firelight from the open grate, was mostly in shadow, with only a few colors glowing strongly. The orange of the cloth under the cat. The dull green beans on the shelf. The red blanket behind the old man in the rocker. The harmonica flashed silver now and then in his hands, and across the room the girl saw a reflection of this in the rippled glass of the windows. The slow chords sounded distant and lonely, and the half-lit room felt to the girl like a small sailing ship bearing the old man and all his worldly goods towards an unknown destination.

She stepped down and crossed to the open doorway and stood looking out, listening to the harmonica. The vast reaches of the thorn trees were shrouded in fog which grew denser and brighter in the distance like a white sea with the waves halted. The nanny stood alone in the center of the yard with her head lifted, gazing out into the pasturage. Nearby, the heavy branches of the oak rocked in the low wind, and the girl looked beyond the tree to the paddock, and saw the blind horse wandering. He moved hesitantly, weaving his head from side to side. Each time he bumped into something—the pump, the trough, the paddock fence— he stopped and thought it over, then continued.

The girl drew the quilt closer around her and went down into the yard and stood near the nanny. The nanny glanced backward quickly, flicking her tail, then gazed outward again at some point in the far distance.

The girl moved closer and put her hand on the goat's neck and looked overhead to where the moon burned steadily through a current of dark clouds. The clouds churned and brightened, transforming themselves into a mantle of huge, smoky roses, and, as she watched them, the girl felt herself rising towards them. The sky began to quicken as if silver dust were spinning through it, and she felt herself moving, weightless, toward some bright center. The air around her was very strong with the smell of roses.

"Mama?" she said.

Then the goat moved under her hand, and the moon was small again behind the smoky clouds, and she stood listening to the harmonica—the slow, drawn-out chords the old man was playing while the cat watched in the dark of the night.

A few hours later, the old man was asleep on the couch, covered with his long black coat. He was dreaming that he lay in a field of crimson poppies surrounded by a turbulence of foot soldiers and horses. The men around him wielded their weapons grimly, with gray faces, and everywhere there was the clank of heavy swords and the thud of horses swerving into each other and the cries of those who had

32

fallen and were being trampled. He, himself, lay on his side, propped up on one elbow, full of the peace of death which he knew was very near. He looked up and saw, bearing down upon him, a big blue-roan horse covered with heavy flaps. Mounted on the horse was a brown-bearded man with eyes full of intense purpose, dressed in coarse vestments and leather. The man was bareheaded, with his hood thrown back, and the skin over his cheeks and throat was as fine as a woman's. He came on steadily, and when he was overhead, and already leaning with easy and amazing power into the swing of the sword, the old man, who was only a young foot soldier, lifted his eyes and exchanged with him a look of forgiveness. Then he accepted the thud of the blade upon his own bone and woke in the cold room to the purring warmth of the cat curled up half asleep on his chest.

He heard the girl crying somewhere upstairs, and he knew from the sharp cold in the room that the fire was long dead. He pushed the cat off him and sat up, frowning and listening. The girl's crying was loud, with a ragged edge to it. He got up and laid back the lid of the stove and filled it hurriedly with wood. He tried to light the kindling but his hands were so cold the matches kept dropping through the grate. Because he couldn't stay away from the girl any longer, he lit the lantern and took it with him up the stairs.

The door to the bedroom stood open. He looked in and saw the covers in a tangle on the bed and a stack of comic books sliding off the pillow. The tapestry-cloth bag rested on the chair beside the chest of drawers. Several blackened matches lay around the lantern, which was empty of oil.

The old man set the lantern on the table and went out into the hall and opened the door into a small airless room at the top of the stairs. He heard the girl make a sound somewhere in there behind the boxes and old broken chairs. He blew into his hands, then took a packet of matches out of his pocket and lit a candle that was set in its own wax on a narrow shelf. He took the candle down, and knelt and held it forward into the shadows, and there was the girl lying on a blanket in a space that she'd made for herself on the floor. Her eyes had a glassy, unseeing look, and she was shivering and biting the back of her hand to keep from crying. The old man blew out the candle. He dragged several boxes out of the way and knelt down by the girl and rolled her over.

"Come on here, now," he said, and he took hold of her by the wrists to haul her up, but she got her hand free and struck him a hard blow on the chest. She gripped the front of his sweater with both hands and whispered, "Wait a minute! Wait a minute!" She drew a long breath and held it, staring unseeing into his face, then let it out in a deep sigh.

The old man wound his hands in the blanket and pulled it and the girl with it out into the hall. Then he took her again by the wrists and lifted her against him. He dragged her by degrees over the threshold and across the bedroom and laid her backwards on the bed. He stripped off the covers and threw the comic books on the floor. The girl lay on her side in the middle of the sheet, trembling. He rolled her over and found that her trousers were tied over her broad belly with a piece of hemp rope. He worked the knot in this loose and hauled the trousers off, and then her underpants, and covered her with the quilt, tucking it securely under the mattress on both sides.

"Your water's broke," he told her, leaning close over her. "It's your time."

"Don't go away again," the girl said, holding onto his arm, but he pulled away from her and went back down the stairs to light the fire.

He had the water boiling in the heavy kettle on the cookstove, and was timing the girl's cries on his pocket watch, which hung in front of him on a nail. He put his pipe between his teeth and struck a match to it, and then unbuttoned his shirt and stripped it off, and then his short-sleeved woolen vest. He dipped a pan into the boiling kettle and poured water from it into the speckled basin on the stand. He soaked a red rag in this hot water and, with the smoke from his pipe in a drift around him, he wetted his chest and soaped himself with a brown bar. He washed vigorously, even his face and his bald head, then dried himself with a flannel rag and pulled on a clean cotton vest.

The cat climbed out of the woodbox and rubbed around his ankles, and looked up at him with a small questioning sound.

"Not this time, General," the old man said.

He took a can of powder down from a shelf over the sink and patted some under his arms and around his neck. Then he picked up from the table an old black doctor's satchel, fastened with brass buckles. He pushed the cat aside gently with his foot and went up the stairs.

The girl let go of the rope which the old man had tied to the bedposts and lay back on the pillows exhausted. Her hair was dark with sweat. She picked up the wet cloth folded beside her pillow and wiped her mouth with it. Then she took a tight hold on two of the old man's fingers.

"Say you wanted to go up-country to the pines by way of the river," she whispered. "Say you was pretty sure you could get you a canoe. It wouldn't take no mor'n a few days, would it?"

She began to tremble and her breath came rapidly again. She reached down for the rope, and the old man put it into her hands. This time when she strained and bore down, she began to shudder violently. The old man turned back the quilt and saw that the child's head was finally visible, a small blue patch of scalp with hair.

The girl lay back and drew her breath in with a ragged gasp and cried, "It's coming! Oh, now, *now* it's coming!"

"Yes, it's coming now," the old man said, throwing the quilt back off the bed. "It's close now."

He set the black satchel on the chest of drawers and unbuckled the straps.

"Help me!" the girl said. "I want to push!"

"Yes," the old man said. "You can push. I'll help you." He

35

put a scalpel into a small curved pan and covered it with alcohol.

"It's coming, now," the girl said, beginning to tremble again. "It's really going to happen, now. Me and you are doing it together, aren't we?"

"Yes," the old man said. He took hold of her ankles and swung them towards him. He turned her until she was crosswise the bed. Then he pulled a chair up close and parted her legs. "Now we are going to work hard together. Do you understand me?"

"Yes," the girl said. "Yes! It's coming now."

"Are you with me, now?" the old man said.

"Yes, I'm with you," the girl said, starting to breathe deeply.

"Are you listening, now?" he said.

"I'm listening," the girl said. "Here it comes. It's coming big this time. So big."

"Bear down!" the old man said.

The girl began to tremble. Her eyes grew wide. "Oh, no," she said. "I can't!"

"Bear down!" the old man shouted, lifting her hands to his neck. "Breathe deep again. That's got it. Now, bear down!"

And the girl pulled against him with the whole of her strength, and fell completely silent, and bore down as if she would never breathe again. While she did this, the child slid slowly out. Then the girl fell back with a long sigh, and the child lay quivering, mottled as marble, just starting to unfold itself in the old man's hands.

The reed basket rested on four bricks laid down on top the cookstove on the warming place. Inside, on a lambswool fleece, lay the child, sucking on one of her fists. She had worked her flannel sheet off into a heap, and now continued to kick first one blue-mottled leg and then the other, jiggling the basket. Nearby, on one of the burners, sat a heavy aluminum saucepan full of bubbling purple broth and beets. Next to this, a cornbread with a quarter cut out of it warmed on a rack.

The cat dozed on the red blanket in the rocker. On a shelf

36

over the counter, a large clock with two big brass alarms ticked loudly next to an old photograph of a young colored woman in a wide, stiff, taffeta dress. Under this shelf, drops of water swelled and fell from the lip of the faucet, tapping on a blue stain in the porcelain sink.

Outside, strong gusts of wind and sleet whipped around the house, making it shudder; but, inside, the room was full of steam, and the sweet aroma of beets, and the smell of cedar wood smoke leaking steadily through the rusted seams of the stovepipe. The room was sealed in, warm and close. Nothing could be seen through the steamed-over windows but the flank of the blind horse, pressed against one of the panes.

Across the yard, on the other side of the cedars, the strong wind drove waves of sleet against the shed, rocking the tin with a sound like thunder. Inside, the old man sat on an upended sorghum pail with his collar turned up, milking the nanny. He had tied her close on the stanchion with a hubcap full of oats under her nose, but she had her head twisted back as far as she could get it, and was chewing softly on his coat, along with the flesh of his shoulder.

The wind stirred the chaff in swirls all around the old man, and flattened the hay in the rack. The nanny raised a hind foot, trying for a good way to get free, but he pressed his forehead into her warm flank and drove the milk steadily through its head of froth.

Behind him, the two kids bleated ceaselessly, staring at him over one rail after another of the dark corner stall.

A short while later, he climbed with the milk pail up into the warm, steamy room, and closed the door hurriedly behind him. He set the pail down on the floor and took off his long black coat and hung it up on a peg. Then he carried the milk across the room and stood looking down into the reed basket with his hand on the rim. The child lay sleeping, her dark head turned to the side. She had long eyelashes and small red lips still pursed from sucking. The skin was translucent over her temples, showing fine blue veins. Her thin legs, spread wide like a frog's, were dwarfed by the thick gray flannel bundle pinned around her buttocks.

"Oh, thou fairest among women," the old man said, "go thy way forth by the footsteps of the flock, and feed thy kids beside the shepherd's tents."

He leaned close over the child and whispered to her.

"We will make thee borders of gold and strands of silver."

He drew the blanket up and folded it in around the edges of the fleece. Then he took a strainer down from a nail and placed this in a wide-mouthed jar in the sink, and poured the milk, with its stiff head of froth, slowly through.

He woke in the deep of the night and looked over at the dark, still shape of the basket on the stove. The wind had died down and the house was very cold. He threw off the coat and sat up on the edge of the couch, swaying a little, listening to the ticking of the large brass clock. He was dressed in his undershirt and trousers with a wool scarf wrapped around his neck and chest.

He unwound the scarf and laid it across the back of the couch and went up the stairs. He stood in the doorway of the bedroom listening to the girl crying softly.

"Margaret," he said, "are you cold?"

"You got it, Granddad," the girl said.

"You want my coat on top of you?"

"No," she said. "I hate that coat."

The old man felt his way through the dark room and stood beside the bed. He could feel the mattress shaking with the girl's shivering.

"How are we going to get you warm?" he said.

"You think you're getting me over to that hospital tomorrow," she said, "But you are going to find out different."

"Child, pay attention to me, now," the old man said. "You are losing too much blood."

"You won't even get me in the car," she said. "You won't even get me down the stairs."

He reached across and found her forehead with his large hand. "Be quiet," he said. He lifted the covers and got in beside her. "Now, come here," he said. He drew her head onto his shoulder and took one of her hands and began to rub the cold out of it.

"You haven't got good sense," he said. "You have got to get sharp, now."

He laid the one hand on his chest and reached for the other.

"You have got to get quiet," he said. "The way a fox lies in the bushes. You have got to get sharp."

The girl couldn't stop shaking. "I don't have to do anything," she said.

"You have got to get through your life, child."

"I don't have to do anything," she said.

The next morning the old man drove into town with the cat sitting beside him in the front seat. The first snow crystals hissed against the glass, and a cold draft blew in under the dashboard, lifting the lapels on the old man's coat and making his eyes water. He drove hunched over, the collar on his coat turned up. The cat sat close beside him, reaching out now and again to bat, with one paw, a brown rabbit's foot that swung on a chain from the key in the ignition.

"We spend our lives as a tale that is told," the old man said. "That's in the Psalms, General." He drove for a while in silence, then pounded the bottom of the steering wheel lightly with his fist and whispered fiercely, "Yes! It's meant to *be!*"

The cat batted at the rabbit's foot, then suddenly, with a whine in his throat, reached up and gathered it into a strong crunch between his jaws. The old man hauled him back by the skin over his shoulder blades and held him in place with the weight of his hand.

"I'll keep the babe until her seventh year," he said. "Until the loss of the milk teeth."

He probed the cat's neck bones gently with his broad fingers.

"She shines so bright," he said softly, "I never saw the like of it."

39

They passed the city limits sign, and the empty stockyards, and the Pleeze-U-Cafe, which at that hour of the morning was closed down with the blinds drawn. Soon they turned onto a dirt track that led uphill to a place where many small cedars stood dark and stiff against the cold November sky. The old man drove through these cedars into a cemetery of old graves. He steered the Studebaker skillfully through the dried weeds until he came to the new section; there he stopped in front of a half-dug grave with a hill of dirt thrown up beside it. He got out, leaving the motor running, and retrieved two shovels and a pick from the ground beside the grave. He put these into the car and got back inside.

"Know whose grave that is?" he said, stroking the cat's back. "It's for Miz Tally Cuthbert, that old lady with the yellow hair that used to drive all the way out to the house every now and then with a tin of peanut brittle. Remember her?" He laughed aloud, rubbing the space between the cat's eyes with his thumb. "Remember that hairnet?" he said. "Remember how she used to shove her false teeth out a little and fall off to sleep in the warm place by the stove? Poor old lady. She said to me, 'Barnabas, I'm counting on you to see me out when the time comes,' and, never knowing I'd have an infant to see to by then, I said, 'Why, Miz Cuthbert, you know I see everybody out.'"

He pressed one of the cat's paws gently between his thumb and forefinger.

"Now they get to call in the boy to finish this grave," he said. "I can't even finish seeing out an old friend."

He put the car in gear and pulled slowly onto the narrow dirt track between the graves.

The girl stood beside the window wrapped in a blanket, watching the snow fall. She had the receiver of the telephone to her ear and was listening to the ringing at the other end.

"Yeah, what is it?" a woman answered. The girl heard music with a heavy beat in the background.

"I want to talk to Montgomery," the girl said.

She heard the receiver being dropped onto the table. "Montgomery!" the woman yelled.

While she waited, the girl watched the snow falling onto the limbs of the oak tree. It fell straight down, vast and quiet. Beyond the tree, the paddock and the cedars were gray shapes, barely discernable.

The old man came down the steps of the municipal building and got into his car. He drove, with the cat beside him, through the center of town. On one side of them were the store fronts, and on the other was the square, with the cement fountain shut off in the center of it and only a few gray, ragged leaves still left on the trees. The Christmas decorations were just going up in town. The old man saw two boys on ladders on opposite sides of the street from one another fastening small, red tinsel trees to the tops of the lampposts.

He steered the Studebaker into an empty parking space in front of the bank, then got out and stood beside the meter, poking through his change purse for a nickel. While he was doing this, a large, red-faced man in a green hunting cap with ear flaps stopped beside him and put a hand on his shoulder.

"Gravedigger, you have *still* got the ugliest car that anybody's ever seen in this county," the man said.

The old man lifted his hat by a small degree and put the nickel in the meter. He waited until the man had slapped him roughly on the shoulder and continued on his way, then he went through the big brass revolving doors into the bank.

The bank president, a cheerful man with cold gray eyes and a big yellow moustache, who had fished the river with the old man many times when they were boys, handed him a peppermint stick out of a box on his desk, and seated him with a pleased look.

"Well Barnabas," he said. "This is an unexpected pleasure. What on earth's the occasion?"

"I've come to sell you my land, Mr. Chamberlin," the old man said. He sat on the edge of his chair holding the peppermint stick straight up like a candle.

The bank president leaned back in his chair and shoved his hands into his pockets. "Well, well," he said. "That takes a moment to sink in, don't it? How much of your land are we talking about here?"

"Why, all of it."

"You're selling *all* your *land?*"

"That is correct."

"What in thunder *for?*"

"Mostly it's for the support of a child," the old man said.

"Barnabas, you old retrograde, I didn't know you had any children."

"I do. I have one child."

"One child. One child. Moving in with its mother, are you?"

"No, Mr. Chamberlin, I'm staying on at the house. That's written into the agreement. I aim to stay on there for seven years."

"That's irregular, Barnabas. What gave you the idea we'd ever agree to that?"

"Well, now, the fact is, my land will square off your parcel over there, won't it?" the old man said. "Aside from the fact there's oil on it."

The bank president jingled the change in his pockets and watched the old man keenly. "Tell me something," he said. "I always wondered. How much do they pay you up yonder on that hill for digging a grave?"

"Twenty-five dollars," the old man said. He studied the heavy gold clock covered with porcelain cherubs resting on the corner of the president's desk. "But mostly I just tend the evergreens," he said.

"How come you to stop being a doctor, Barnabas?"

"I lost one too many patients."

"Lose a lot of patients, did you?"

"No. Just one."

"You going to be able to *live* on twenty-five dollars a grave through your old age, Barnabas?"

"I don't think I'll be digging any more graves, Mr. Chamberlin."

"Tell me truly, now. Are you up to something foolish?"

"I don't think so."

"You haven't got a woman, have you?"

"Not a very large one."

"You couldn't *take* a large one, Barnabas," the president said, and laughed warmly over this joke, then grew suddenly sober.

"One of these days you're going to really *need* this capital, Barnabas," he said. "You people are all like children. Throwing your money away on anything bright and shiny. No thought for the morrow."

"Nothing can be done with us, though, you've always said so."

"Yes, I have."

"Put your finger right on it," the old man said. He stood up and took a thick envelope out of his pocket and laid it on the inkblotter of the president's desk. "Here are the papers. I believe they're in order. All you've got to give it is your signature."

The bank president took a small, hard eyeglass case out of an inside pocket of his jacket. He lifted his glasses out and slipped the wire rims carefully over one ear at a time, then leaned forward and slid the papers out of the envelope. He glanced quickly over the first page.

"Sad," he said, reaching for his pen.

The old man got out of the car in the thickly falling snow. He crossed over a small wooden footbridge and opened the latch on a blue gate and went under a trellis of winter-brown wisteria. As he walked up the concrete path, bordered on both sides by rustling spears of dead zinnias, a large, shiny-skinned colored woman of middle years opened the door and came out to meet him. She was running a long hat pin through a red mesh covering the rolls of her hair, and she had on red shoes and a flower-print dress with rhinestone buttons and a long, stiff, muskrat coat. She came down the steps gingerly in her high heels and walked up to the old man and gave him a hard jab on the breastbone.

"Fool!" she said. She hit him on the arm with her handbag. "Addle-brain!"

The old man took out his wallet and thumbed through its contents, counting, while the large flakes of snow settled on his hat and shoulders. He took out a number of bills and folded them and put them into her purse. "I had a list here, somewhere," he said, patting his pockets. He found, in his trousers, a piece of paper the size of a matchbox. "Ten diapers," he read off of it. "One bar of Fels Naptha. One rubber duck."

"You are pitifully afflicted," the woman said. She took the slip away from him and tore it into several pieces. "They finished your head without the brains," she said. She turned and went on towards the gate.

"Safety pins!" The old man called out. "That was on there, too." But the woman paid him no mind. She slammed the gate behind her, turning towards the store fronts that could be seen at a distance down the road. She headed off through the blowing snow at a good pace, pitched slightly forward on her high heels. When she reached the corner, a gust of wind hit her, blowing her coat open and pushing her off course into the weeds, but she clamped a hand over her hairnet and kept on going.

"I'll be over to pick everything up tomorrow morning early!" the old man called loudly, but the woman was out of earshot by then and never looked back.

The old man drove home slowly, peering carefully through the blowing walls of snow. The brown cat slept soundly beside him, the claws of one paw hooked slightly in the leg of his trousers.

When he came to his own road, he was surprised to see

the gate standing open and the horse gone. He got out of the car and stood in the open gateway, calling, "Blue! Blue!" into the strong wind, but the horse never appeared.

He drove down the long track and pulled into the yard. In front of him, around the trunk of the oak tree, rested many severed branches. His chainsaw lay out in the open ground, flattened in the middle, as if it had been run over. He looked beyond this scene and studied the house, which was dark, with the front door standing open. He got out of the car and hauled the pick out of the front seat with trembling hands, and then stepped backwards into a tangle of barbed wire that had been dragged up across the road. He dropped the pick and sought to yank the wire off his trousers, but more rolls of it slapped up against him, catching onto his sleeves. He sat down and took a long time pulling the wire off him strand by strand, then crawled away from it on his hands and knees.

A moment later he stepped up into the house and stood looking at the overturned cookstove which rested on its face, emptying many small hills of ashes out onto the floor. The blue jars full of beets had been thrown with force against the walls, and the room was covered with shards of purple glass. Beside him, on the floor, he saw one of his rosewood radios half buried in a drift of snow.

He went upstairs and looked through the empty rooms there, then came down and stepped out under the porch roof. He heard the nanny calling incessantly from the direction of the cedars, and he crossed the yard, bending into the wind, and entered the trees. He wandered there a long time, lost among the dark shapes of the cedars, aware of the fragrance of the reddish brown chaff being scuffed up under his boots. Finally the wind died down and he left the cedars and found the nanny tied to a post in the corner of the paddocks. She was bound very close. She'd wound the tether around herself and the post tighter than the lace in a shoe.

Not far off, the two kids lay on their sides, a foot apart, in the center of the paddock. Their legs were twisted under them and their necks turned back. The snow under them was darkly stained.

The old man knelt down beside the nanny, who was charged with trembling, with wildness, and tried to unbind her, but the rope was tight as a cable. He took his knife out of his pocket and opened the blade, and then he laid his face against hers and stroked her long, narrow throat.

"Nefertiti," he whispered, "so slender in her bracelets. Swimming pale as ivory in the reeds along the river."

He brought his arm around her and slipped the knife carefully under the rope.

The blunt-nosed, rusty, red car entered the town at dusk, emitting a deafening noise through the muffler along with blue sparks and clouds of foul-smelling exhaust. The person on the street at that hour most attracted to the sound of this car was a small boy with a shaved head who sat hunched over on the bench in front of the liquor store with his hands thrust into the pockets of his thin nylon jacket. The boy watched the car turn slowly onto the main street in the quietly falling snow. It came steadily on towards him, passing under the garlands of colored lights and tinsel, driving before it a big white horse attached to the bumper by a length of frayed rope.

The car cruised slowly along the darkening street, throbbing with the heavy beat of its radio, attracting the notice of a few people who went to the curb to watch it as it passed. Its windshield was blanketed with snow except for the two small funnels under the wipers. An arm in a black leather jacket hung from the open window of the passenger's side, clutching a bottle of beer.

The car made its way steadily through the center of town, taking no notice of the traffic light, and pulled up in front of the liquor store, which was just shutting off its neon sign. The motor was left running while the back door of the car swung open and a pinch-faced Mexican boy wearing a red rayon shirt and thin, shiny black shoes, stepped out, shivering, into the gray sludge. "Mother of God," he said under his breath. He made a quick, obscene signal for the benefit of the small boy on the bench, and hurried, hunched over and freezing, through the door of the liquor store.

The small boy studied the white horse which stood in front of the car with its head down, covered with dark sweat and froth. He heard a baby crying somewhere, and he looked through the windshield wipers and saw a small, black, rubber head with its eyes closed and its lips stitched shut hanging from the rear view mirror. He watched the black leather arm hurl the beer bottle against the brick front of the store, and then he heard someone laugh shrilly and say, "You hear that, Montgomery? Little sister in the back here wants us to take her up-country to the pine trees. How much gas we got left in the tank?"

The white horse let its breath out in a long sigh, and the boy on the bench looked over and saw, for the first time, the strange, milky-blue pupils of its eyes. He dropped down off the bench and crossed over and put his hand under its nose to feel its warm breath. Then he slipped the rope-noose forward over its head.

"Bet I'm going to catch heck," he said, giving the horse a shove on the shoulder.

He stood in front of the car a long time with the rope in his hand, listening to the windshield wipers and the heavy beat from the radio, watching the horse move off slowly into the snow.

Shiny Objects

Mrs. Gillnetter was a dark, serious-looking person. Her hands, folded in her lap, were blunt and rough. Small, hard muscles showed in her arms from years of work. A heavy grayness hung under her eyes and around her mouth, as if she lived on food without any taste to it and was deaf to all musical sound. She had hardly moved in more than an hour, only once securing in her coarse black hair the two small tortoise-shell combs, sharp as cats' teeth, that fastened her braids.

She sat on the porch in a wicker rocker, looking down the long dirt track that led from her house to the road. Before yesterday, when Mr. Cunningham had spent the entire afternoon in her parlor, nobody but herself had traveled up that track in over a year.

On a wire directly in front of her sat a quivering blue-and-rust-colored swallow. Clean, dark fire flashed from its eyes. It glanced back and forth between Mrs. Gillnetter and a river-mud nest with four eggs in it under the eaves.

Over Mrs. Gillnetter's head, an old wide-spreading locust, dense with bees, rubbed its flowering branches mournfully across the roof, and nearby, at the edge of the yard, a band of sheep with two new lambs ranged along the wire fence. One of these sheep, though it stayed close with the others and gave no evidence of suffering any particular problem, had been bleating monotonously all morning.

Though the springtime was in full progress all around her, Mrs. Gillnetter gave no thought to it. She was awaiting the arrival of a child, a boy of twelve. She had been informed, by means of a fat letter stuffed with medical records, that this child was in need of special care and that the county would pay her handsomely for taking him. She had never seen him, and she disliked everything Mr. Cunningham had told her about him in her parlor yesterday afternoon.

"I am not exaggerating," Mr. Cunningham had said, "when I tell you that we're speaking here of an individual who spends every waking hour rewriting the Bible."

Mrs. Gillnetter didn't hold with the Bible. She found all the turbulence in it upsetting, and she doubted whether any amount of attention given to it by a twelve-year-old boy, who was himself in need of special care, was going to lighten it up any.

Mr. Cunningham had shown her a photograph in which all she could make out clearly was a wide dead-white face set directly onto a pair of frail shoulders, the eyes in shadow under a shelf of dark hair. Later, along with her copy of the child-care papers, Mrs. Gillnetter had thrown this photograph into the oil drum out back and burned it. She'd indicated on the form they'd given her to fill out in the beginning that she wanted a teenage girl. Now this sickly-looking boy with an overlarge head was due to arrive at any moment. Mrs. Gillnetter felt as if the county people had her by the wrists and around the waist, and were rushing her against her will into an ugly situation.

"You got nobody but yourself to blame," she said aloud to herself, by which she meant that when Mr. Cunningham had squatted spread-legged on a stool yesterday afternoon, carrying on about the boy and showing off his photograph, she, for her part, had only sat staring at the oval rug with pansies on it lying on the floor between them and had said nothing. It was always that way. While she was casting about for the right words to express her feelings, the other person always ran off with the decision.

She recalled that Mr. Cunningham had smelled like a lemon-meringue pie that had been left out too long in the room. He was a stout man, dressed in a white summer suit and a string tie secured by a knob of turquoise as big as a turkey egg. He had stood over her, mopping his neck with a red kerchief, while she worked on the papers.

"The boy's full name is Ulysses Montgomery Dade," he had said, leaning so close over her that she nearly stopped

50

breathing. "But take your time, Miss Lucy. We got all the time in the world."

She always got so angry she could hardly control herself whenever anybody called her Lucy, but instead of strangling Mr. Cunningham by hauling backwards with sudden and unexpected force on his string tie like she wanted to, she had excused herself and gone and stood for a long time in the pantry with her arms rolled up in her apron.

Now she looked down the dirt track once more and caught sight of a man in a fedora hat standing at the gate. This man was so short that he was obliged to hang from the top board by both hands. Mrs. Gillnetter perceived on this person some sort of footgear, shaped like two black leather buckets, that was unfamiliar to her. She thought to herself, studying this apparition, that it never failed that if you already had one thing to deal with on a particular afternoon, there was always bound to come along another.

She went to the edge of the porch steps and called out, "You'd best go on now. This here isn't any place to be waiting around." The man continued to peer at her through the bars, making no move to leave. She looked closely at him and made out a pair of thick, rimless glasses under the fedora hat and a mustard-colored heavy woolen suit. Resting under the gate, in the dust of the track, were an old black satchel and a cardboard box tied shut with hemp rope. "Looks like some kind of dwarf salesman has run out of gas," Mrs. Gillnetter said.

"Mr. Gillnetter and I don't have any gas right now," she called out, "but down the next house is a telephone."

"I know you ain't married," the person at the gate called out to her, and this made her immediately so angry that she had to turn and go inside the house.

She continued the next half hour to keep watch through the front windows. On about the seventeenth time she went to do this, she was relieved to see that the dwarf was gone. "It always pays to just go on about your life," Mrs. Gillnetter said, and then the telephone rang.

51

"Miss Lucy, I'm afraid there is going to be maybe a short delay," Mr. Cunningham said to her on the phone. "There is no sense making up a story to you about it, the boy has received the bad news this morning that his condition is terminal, and it was temporarily upsetting to him, and now he has run off."

While she was having this conversation with Mr. Cunningham in her kitchen, she was able to see, through the window over the sink pump, a short boy with an overlarge head climbing into the back of the blue and green Plymouth truck that had rested unused beside the tractor shed for fourteen years. The boy hauled the black satchel and the cardboard box with him up into the truck and went and sat down with his back against the cab. Mrs. Gillnetter watched him take off his heavy glasses and wipe them carefully on a fold in his shirtfront and put them back on, adjusting the delicate wires over his ears one at a time. Then he sat with his arms around the satchel, fanning off blue-bottle flies with his battered fedora.

Mrs. Gillnetter laid the phone down gently on the counter while Mr. Cunningham was still talking and went out onto the screen porch and stood there watching the boy. Before long, he appeared to come to a decision. He took off his jacket, climbed down out of the truck and disappeared into the shed. He emerged a few moments later dragging out a small bedsprings. As he hauled this bedsprings through the dust of the yard, Mrs. Gillnetter was able to see for the first time that his legs were strongly bowed and that his feet were tilted to the sides, which action had caused the black leather buckets with their heavy laces to run down over the soles.

Mrs. Gillnetter felt safe on the screen porch. She sat on a stack of newspapers that she had collected there and began to cast about for the right words to express her feelings to the county people. "I am not equipped," she said to them in a whisper.

The boy struggled for a long time getting the bedsprings up into the truckbed, then returned to the shed and dragged out the mattress. This narrow bed was the very one Mrs. Gillnetter had slept on as a child, and she wondered if he was going to set up the wooden-spool bedstead in the back of the truck, too. She remembered that she had been waked in that bed every morning of the world by a black and white terrier named Gabriel that used to stand on her chest licking her face until she threw him off.

"That dog is long dead," she said. She began to search for the words to tell the boy that he would not be staying.

While she was doing this, he went several times back into the shed. He brought out a lacquer-paper Chinese screen, a table-top with bluebirds stenciled onto it, a coat rack, a stack of horse blankets, and an old, leaded, green glass window. He arranged these belongings carefully, with many pauses and considerations, in the back end of the truck.

The sun was getting down low over the fields, making long shadows, when Mrs. Gillnetter opened the screen door and went outside. She crossed the yard slowly with her arms wrapped up in her apron and stopped under a persimmon tree a few feet away from the boy. He sat on the mattress, writing on an Indian Head tablet that he had in his lap. There were maybe two dozen wadded-up balls of yellow paper lying around him, and his hair showed clearly that he'd been running his fingers every which way through it. He wore a look of turbulence as if he were possessed by thoughts not meant to be conjured up together. He glanced at her with his eyes full of dark feeling and reached for the fedora, pulling it very low to the front. From the shadow under the brim, he studied her with a strong direct gaze.

"You a Mexican?" he asked.

She didn't answer him.

"You colored?"

"You have got to go back," she said. "I am very sorry for the inconvenience."

"There wouldn't be no problem with that," the boy said, "except that I have moved in here."

"No, you have not," she said.

"Yes. I saw it in a dream."

Mrs. Gillnetter unrolled her arms from her apron and moved out of the shadow of the persimmon tree. She felt the orange color from the late sun slant over her, filling her with a wellspring of beauty and power that came seldom to her. "You think you are big enough that you can work it so you get your way, only you are not," she said. "You are only a puny child."

The boy swung his strange leather boots over the edge of the mattress and stood up, bracing himself with a hand on the coat rack, and Mrs. Gillnetter was startled to see that he was about as tall as an eight-year-old child.

"I am a new voice," he said.

"You are a dwarf child without so much as a penny nor any place to live, and you had better take heed that you are at the mercy of strangers," Mrs. Gillnetter said.

"You are at the mercy of the stranger, too," the boy said.

He took off the fedora and came a step forward, emerging out of the shadows, and when Mrs. Gillnetter looked at his face turned full towards her, she felt as if a deep, sad, far-off note had rung from a bell, turning the late evening light and the sheep at the fence and the dark trees churning softly in the wind into something far other than she had all these years perceived.

"The stranger," the boy said. "The thief. He has come into your household even now for gold."

Mrs. Gillnetter rolled her arms back up in her apron. She went a step nearer. They remained that way for a while, like two solitary people thrown together suddenly on a journey, the dwarf child in the truck and the woman on the ground, looking at each other in genuine affliction and alarm.

That evening Ulysses Montgomery carried all his furniture into the house and up the stairs and locked himself away in a room on the second floor. In the days following, the total silence, combined with Mrs. Gillnetter's unwillingness to knock on the door, caused her many vexations of the spirit. She abandoned as hopeless several schemes to evict the child from her house, progressing from these to the possibility of going to live in a hotel she had once stayed at in Sweetwater, which had a small room over the back stairwell that was shut off altogether from the traffic. She left the boy food at mealtimes on a tray with a cross-stitch napkin over it outside his door, but he never touched it.

On the afternoon of the third day, she heard him singing about pomegranates. She was in the kitchen, scalding a chicken. She heard the song through a grate in the ceiling over her head. After the song about pomegranates, he began a song about cinnamon and grapes. While he was singing this song, Mrs. Gillnetter became aware of energetic flapping, and a full-grown crow appeared at the window over the sink pump, causing her to drop the pullet off the fork into the scalding water, which splashed up over the edge and half drenched the fire. She stood, with the fork in one hand and the lid to the scalding pot in the other, watching the crow, which seemed as if it were appearing to her in a dream. It strode back and forth along the windowsill, putting its head first to one side and then the other. In the tip of its beak it held a small silver star. It dropped the star through a hole in the screen, looked in keenly after it, then flew away.

"Give a crow a shiny object," Mrs. Gillnetter said.

She went to the window and looked inside the sill. She saw a tarnished tin star lying there. She lifted the edge of it with a prong of the fork, but it was as homely and blank on one side as it was on the other. She looked out of the window at the persimmon tree, which had dark leaves pointing upward crisply and a multitude of small purple-throated flowers. This tree seemed to her, like the crow, as if it were about to speak to her out of a dream. A pale blue fire stirred the air around it. Mrs. Gillnetter studied this for a while, then turned back into the kitchen to relight the stove.

Late that evening, she put away everything in the kitchen and scrubbed the table with a coarse brush and a sprinkling of salt. She took the bucket of ashes outdoors, and spread them evenly among her onions. Then she went upstairs to where the boy was locked away in his room and spoke to him for the first time.

"I'm not bringing no more food up here to this door," she said.

She heard his heavy dragging step approach and stop close by.

"Food?" he said.

"That's right. And I am not equipped for no more conjuring, neither."

"What food?" the boy said.

"Why, the food I have brought up here three times a day."

"There's food there?"

"Not no more, there ain't."

"Where'd it go?"

"Where'd it go? Why, I took it back down again."

"Well, say what it was. Was it yams? And parsnips? And nut meats? And the whole business melted over with brown sugar?"

"Pshaw, boy! It was *food*. Regular *food*."

"Was it barley cakes? Stuffed with raisins, maybe, and pork and pineapple?"

Mrs. Gillnetter, finding it tedious to go on with this conversation, fell silent. The boy opened the door and stood before her, barefoot and bare-chested in his heavy woolen suit.

"Are you playing tricks on me about the food?" he said. His eyes were bright with pain.

"You have got grit to say that," Mrs. Gillnetter said. "You with your devil crows. You with your fiery trees."

The boy lowered his head and moved, with a dragging step, out into the hall towards the stairs.

"I have to go find food, now," he said.

"Not in my kitchen, you don't," Mrs. Gillnetter said.

She hurried past him on the stairs and went into the kitchen and bolted the door. After a moment, she heard him go out the front, and she stood in the middle of the darkening kitchen, thinking maybe he had left, maybe he was headed out to the road intent on returning to the county home; but then she heard a scratch on the window screen, and turning, saw him looking in at her, his large head dark against the red of the late evening sky. The sight of him made her suddenly very angry. She took off her apron and flapped it at him and rushed toward the window, calling, "Shush, now! Shush!" She beat on the screen, seeking to drive him away, but he was intent on getting in. He forced his fingers around the edges of the screen and rattled it in its frame. The sound of his labored breathing, coming from so close in the darkness, was alarming. Mrs. Gillnetter could just make out the dark fire in his eyes.

She went around the unlit kitchen swiftly, closing all the windows, after which she sat down at the table, trembling. She took up, from the center of the table, the small red rooster that held the pepper, and set to polishing his head with her apron.

The boy had disappeared momentarily into the night. Suddenly Mrs. Gillnetter heard a pounding like thunder along the bottom of the sill.

"He has got hold of a fair-sized stone," she said. She set the rooster down again beside the white hen and folded her hands in her lap.

The pounding progressed from window to window, and after a while Mrs. Gillnetter could take no more of it. She got a plate off the shelf and went to the cooler and took out chicken and butter. She brought out greens and black-eyed peas and mixed these with vinegar and a little pork fat in the skillet. She blew a fire up under a handful of faggots, and warmed the boy's food over the direct flame.

He was taking the screen door off its hinges when she got to the back porch. She opened the inside door the space of its chain and called through.

"You listen here to me, now," she said. "It's only the lowest kind of animal behaves that-a-way outside the house."

"How come you to shut me out?" he said. "I can't abide it. I can't abide it, hear?"

"Now quit!" Mrs. Gillnetter said, "and sit right there on that stair."

But the boy went down the steps and disappeared in the dark yard. Soon she heard him come in the front and go up the stairs to his room. He shut the door with a crash, throwing the bolt loudly, and drew something heavy against it.

"No telling what will happen now," Mrs. Gillnetter said.

She went out onto the porch and stood looking into the darkness, the plate with the food on it growing cold in her hand.

"How quick it all comes up, without no warning," she said. "Land, it's like when we was little, and it would be a sunshiny day, with nothing untowards at all, and then one of the hands would holler out. 'Better head home, chil'ren, they's wolves sighted on the far hill.'"

She set the plate of food down at the top of the steps and peered into the night.

"Black as pitch," she said.

Towards midnight the moon rose, and Mrs. Gillnetter lay awake in the light of it for a long while, troubled with sleeplessness and indecision. Finally, she got up out of bed and went to the door of the boy's room and knocked on it sharply.

"Tomorrow morning early I am going to take a screwdriver to the hinges on this door," she called out.

After a moment she heard the sound of the bedsprings and the laboring commotion the boy made when he got to his feet. Soon the latch was lifted and the door opened. Ulysses Montgomery stood before her, squinting in the harsh light from the hallway, barely awake. He was clad only in his undershorts, and his naked legs were startling in their deformity. His head, which he carried laid back slightly, appeared to burden him with its weight, and his chest was like an old peach basket with the ribs sprung. The frailty of the whole of him gave Mrs. Gillnetter suddenly an entirely new feeling about him. She reached past him and pulled the door closed gently and waited there in the hall, listening. She heard no sound whatever. She pictured him leaning with his forehead against the doorsill, fast asleep. After a moment, she turned out the light and went back to bed.

She had slipped away into a dream in which she was crossing over a wide bridge together with a multitude of people, when she woke to find Ulysses Montgomery standing beside her in the moonlight.

"You scared?" he asked her.

She raised herself up on her elbow and peered at him. He looked at her as if they had been in conversation most of the night and had only just that moment reached a mutual conclusion.

"Well, I am," he said. He turned and disappeared into the dark. She heard him dragging his feet over the floorboards, through the hall, down the stairs.

Mrs. Gillnetter lay back on her pillows. For the second time that night, she was overcome by the hugeness of her misfortune. Memory pictures of all that had happened since she first caught sight of the boy at her gate assaulted her out of the darkness. She thought back to the way her life had been before he had come. The long days of the locust limbs creaking, and the wash on the line billowing in the sun. The great banks of clouds appearing out of one quarter of the sky and disappearing soundlessly into another. The gentle changes in the light. The stars at night so dense in their mantle. And then she'd started all that business connected with the teenage girl and had finally, God forgive her, written the letter to the county people. What foolishness. Where was that girl now?

A memory came over her suddenly of the blissful feeling she had had all those years ago after Mr. Gillnetter left. She remembered taking deep sighs day after day, the peace and gladness which no words could circumscribe. That feeling had stayed with her, true and unchanging through all the years of solitude.

In the midst of these thoughts, she heard the screen door on the back porch open and clatter shut.

"Now he has gone out of the house in the middle of the night," she said.

She got up and looked out the window, and there was Ulysses Montgomery crossing the yard in the moonlight. He moved haltingly without his shoes. She watched him cross, with his dragging step, between the trough and the windmill.

"He is headed out into the pasturage," she said.

She went down the stairs with her nightgown in a billow around her and sat on the stack of newspapers on the porch and laced on her boots.

"He is going to get caught in the cactus," she said.

She took the lantern from the nail. After lighting it, she put the matches in her pocket. She let the screen door slam and crossed the yard swiftly. The circle of light from the lantern swung violently around her as she went under the barbed wire. Beyond the fence began the vast expanse of prickly-pear cactus and mesquite.

Soon she saw Ulysses Montgomery ahead of her, dragging his feet laboriously over the rough ground. He kept on at the same pace, looking straight ahead, even when the light from the lantern slipped over him. When she caught up with him, she could think of nothing whatever to say and was forced to walk slowly alongside of him, stumbling over stony ground, getting her nightgown caught repeatedly in the pricklebush and thistles.

Finally, he stopped.

"This here's the top of the rise," he said.

Mrs. Gillnetter looked around her. She couldn't see as they were at the top of anything. The land was as flat as a griddle.

"Put that thing out," he said, and he took hold of the lantern before she could do anything about it and blew out the flame. When he did this, the night sky with its stars became a bowl over them.

"Over yonder in that direction is the river they call the Jordan which flows into the Sea of Galilee," he said. "All acrost the holy land is olive trees and fields of wheat growing and poppy flowers. I saw it in a picture."

He swung the unlit lamp slowly forward. "And that-a-way lies the polar ice cap which is all over miles deep with ice as blue as any diamond. They's whole mountains of ice moving by slow degree towards the sea."

He set the lantern on the ground between them.

"And over there. Know what's over there?" he said.

Mrs. Gillnetter knew what lay in that direction. It was a road that led to the home of a friend who had long ago deserted her. Looking across the moonlit trees toward that road, Mrs. Gillnetter saw this woman clearly as she had been when they were both young, the abundant chestnut hair held back in a ribbon, the narrow lace collar closed with an abalone pin.

"It's a no-account place without even a church," she said, thinking of the town where the other woman still lived.

"China," Ulysses Montgomery said. "That-a-way lies China. It's all the wonders you can imagine. Gold and silver ships, and lakes with swans, and streets paved with ivory and jasper. Only no man has ever seen it. Not ever. It all lies beyond a wall no man has ever climbed."

Mrs. Gillnetter was picturing the abalone pin lying on velvet in the small drawer of her dresser. Abruptly, she picked up the lantern.

"It's too far out here for us to be standing about dreaming on such things," she said. She took the matches from her pocket and lit the lantern and held it up between them. They looked at each other in silence. "There's cattle out here," she said.

"And snakes, too, probably," Ulysses Montgomery said.

"Yes, snakes, too," she said.

"I wished I was a snake."

Mrs. Gillnetter was forced against her will to laugh. "That's some kind of low life," she said.

"Yes, a snake has been consigned low," he said. "He has been consigned so low he can't never lift up any part of hisself off the ground, only his head. He don't have any power to laugh nor anything to laugh at. So how can Jesus love him? Why, he loves him *because* he can't fly. He loves him him *because* he can't sing. He loves him because he has intimate knowledge of everything from having to crawl *over* it."

Mrs. Gillnetter studied Ulysses Montgomery in the lantern light. His limbs were sunken over the long bones and swollen at the joints. There were hollows under his eyes. He looked as frail and spongy as a tumbleweed. She couldn't imagine where he had got the strength to come this far out into the pasturage.

"No chance you'll make it back," she said.

The boy's face, which had been bright until that moment, went dull and tired suddenly. He looked at the ground. "You're right, there," he said. "I have ruint my feet for this night. I can't walk no more tonight."

Mrs. Gillnetter looked back towards the house, wishing she'd left on a light. She could just make out the windmill fluttering, small and far away.

"How are we going to get you back?" she said.

"You are going to carry me," he said.

She felt a wave of sickness come over her at the mention of this. She looked away from him.

"Give me that thing," he said, taking the lantern. He stood sideways to her. "Ain't nothing for it only to just go ahead with it," he said. "Nobody ever minds it too much after the first time."

She bent and caught him under the knees and around the ribs. She had never carried anybody before, not even an infant. When she felt him fold against her, like a bird drawing its wings in, she caught sight, suddenly, of something very like the whole of his life. It was as if he had pulled his life in with him so small and compact and vivid that it could almost be put into her pocket.

She carried him carefully over the stony ground. The lantern, swinging in front of them, cast great shadows dancing from the trees. She was amazed at the feel of him, the smallness of his bones.

He held very still and didn't look up, but after a while he said to her, "What would you be for an animal?"

"I don't hold with all that," she said.

"A fish," he said. The hand holding the lantern sank lower, and she felt his head lean heavily against her. "You are a fish. In the waters. In amongst the bread." He spoke in a whisper.

She was able to take the lantern from him before it slipped down. He was very still as they crossed under the low trees, and she thought he was asleep, but after a moment he began to meddle with the long braid that had come forward over her shoulder. He unwound the strands of it.

"I wouldn't keep on with that," she said.

But he pulled the braid loose into the heavy waves that she never liked to live with except for the time it took to brush them, and he drew the mass of her hair forward and lifted his head onto it and wound his hand in it.

"Feeding on the bread," he said, his voice so low that she could barely hear.

Soon his breathing was steady, warm on her neck, and she knew by the subtle change in the weight of him that he was asleep.

Where the Water Is Wide

The old road bent neither to the left nor right. The deaf girl drove the truck through the darkness with William Henry Grover, who was eight years old, sitting beside her in his cowboy outfit. They stared straight ahead at the sweep of dry brush and cactus picked up by the headlights, enjoying a feeling of restfulness and safety. The space around them was lit by the green lights on the dashboard, and smelled of aging foam-rubber and chocolate and oily rags.

The deaf girl had fine red hair and a wide forehead and dark blue eyes that looked dreamy and strange. She wore a flower-print dress and sneakers the color of newspaper that's been lying out in the rain.

William Henry Grover was a large-headed child, with heavy eyebrows under his cowboy hat and very short legs.

The deaf girl reached over and turned on the radio. She saw William Henry's boots begin to bob rhythmically, and soon he was swaying back and forth with his head thrown back, singing along with the music. After a while he rummaged around in the big shopping bag with handles on it that she always carried with her, and brought out a twist of licorice. He broke off two whips which he laid across his knee. The rest, rolled into a ball the size of his fist, he stuffed in his shirt.

The deaf girl's name was Angel. William Henry's parents, who traveled with a country and western band, had brought her in to live with them when she was nine and William Henry was a baby. Recently they'd taught her how to drive the truck in case William Henry, who had sugar diabetes, had to be driven to the hospital while they were away from home. Now Angel and William Henry always had a pleasurable time in the evenings. They drove the truck into town and parked it in the alley behind the Hickey Brothers Superette and went exploring through the dark neighborhoods, looking in at people through their windows.

It had begun to rain in a fine drizzle. When they came into town they saw that everyone had taken refuge in the Pleeze-U-Cafe, which was brightly lit, with many cars parked in front of it. The deaf girl leaned forward and looked through streaks of rain on the glass. When they were past the cafe, she saw a man standing in the next block in front of a dark store window. The man was dressed neatly in a white shirt and tie. He was just standing in the rain looking in through the window. His jacket, hanging from his hand, dragged on the wet pavement. When she was even with him, she saw he was a deaf man she knew who owned a store on Main Street. She always stayed away from him because as soon as he saw her he would try to talk to her with his hands. His way of doing this was always too urgent, like being in a current, in a river, that was too strong to cross.

She drove past the man and turned the corner, and when she had gone around the block she saw him standing further up the street under a lamp. She pulled the truck to the curb and turned off the ignition. William Henry touched her on the wrist, but she shook her head, watching the man. His hair was plastered down with the rain. He stepped out of the circle of light and crossed the street, and she got down out of the truck and began to follow him. She had not gone far before William Henry caught up with her, and she took his hand.

The man turned onto a side street. After several blocks the sidewalk ended, and the man and the deaf girl and William Henry walked in the road through a dark neighborhood of small, rather shabby houses. The yards had patches of gravel showing through the brown grass. They had chinaberry trees growing in them, and arbor vitae and crepe myrtle, and now and then a large pecan tree with the nuts lying on the ground under it like small green turtles. Many of the houses were sided with asbestos shingles. One house

66

had a bright outside light shining from one corner, and, as they approached, the deaf girl watched the drizzle fall through this light, and when they were even with the house she saw a large white dog lying chained on the ground beside the porch. The dog lifted its head, watching them intently as they passed.

The man went into a house that was almost hidden under a magnolia tree. The deaf girl walked under the tree and looked up at the big white flowers glistening and ghostly among the black leaves. She made William Henry stay with her a long time under the tree, waiting for a light to go on in the house, but it remained dark. Finally she went into the yard. She took a tablet from the shopping bag and wrote on it, "The peace which passeth all understanding shall keep your heart and mind." She put this note into the mailbox in front of the house and took William Henry's hand and they walked back up the road the way they had come. When they passed the house with the light, they looked for the white dog, but he was gone. There was a circle of hard earth with a chain lying in it where he had been.

Later that night it stopped raining. The sky cleared. Out in the countryside the stars crowded close with a vast booming sound and the moon shed an intense light on clumps of prickly pear and sleeping sheep. After midnight, when all the lights were extinguished in the Pleeze-U-Cafe, the town was dark. For a long time the moon shone in at the window on the deaf man asleep in his bed. It shone brightly on his exhausted face. Often he stirred fitfully as if he were trying to swim in the tangled sheets, and his hands kept shifting and signaling through the night.

Carl Gottlieb was a deaf man, in the middle of his life. He had a rather flat face with eyes that glittered in irritation whenever anyone distracted him from his thoughts. He was strong, thick through the chest, brooding and dark. On his long nightly walks through the town, he strode forward heavily, with his head down, his hands forming an occasional brief sign in front of his chest.

He lived alone in a quiet neighborhood. Beside his small brown stucco house grew an old magnolia tree which all through the summer was full of giant white flowers. At night these flowers, luminous among the black leaves, penetrated his dreams with their fragrance.

He worked in his garden every summer evening. He liked to stand in it with the hose, soaking the soil around the vegetables while the evening deepened around him. He would stay until it was completely dark, until the light had retreated into a gold ribbon hovering close over the horizon.

He owned a drygoods store, located on the main street of the town. A door at the back of the store led into a low room in which the air was thick with the sweet odor of hides. The room held three long tables piled high with heavy skins. Cut strips littered the floor and lay in mounds in the corners. The smaller pelts—lynx and ferret and fox—were kept in cupboards on the walls.

One day, late in the summer, Carl sat in this room, cutting rawhide thongs. Over his knees lay a fox pelt—a silver fox with the head and paws still on it. Sometimes, when no one was in the store, he liked to open his shirt and put this particular pelt next to his skin. He liked to flatten it out over his chest and ribs and wear it like that for hours with his shirt buttoned over it.

Now he sat on a stool, with the fox pelt on his knees, cutting thongs from a cowhide with heavy, blunt scissors. The strips of leather lay around him on the floor.

When he saw the red light go on, which meant he had a customer, he threw the pelt onto the table in irritation and went into the store with the scissors still in his hand. He found a woman there that he never liked to deal with. She was a small woman, weatherbeaten as an old mesquite tree. Winter and summer, she wore the same felt hat and soiled jacket. She was always quietly drunk.

When Carl handed her the tablet and pencil, she took the

last inch of a brown cigarette from her lips and held it carefully between her knuckles while she wrote.

My well has gone dry, Carl.

He read this, then handed the tablet back to her and waited.

Also, them dogs have got round to my place now.

He shrugged and wrote on the tablet – *You want?*

She took the tablet from him and bent over it tensely, forming the letters with care.

Have you got a trap that catches a dog but don't kill it?

Carl answered her – *This is foolish and sentimental. For dogs we have poison. That is what we have.*

He went behind the counter and took down a cannister of poison and set it in front of her. She shook her head and started to write something more, but he came out and took the tablet away and pointed to the door. The woman hesitated, looking uncertain about what should be done, but finally she turned and went out.

After Carl put the poison back on the shelf, he looked through the front window and saw the girl. She was sitting on the bench by the curb with the small boy she always had with her. When she turned her head, the line of her cheek caused something to tighten under his breastbone. He studied her white forehead, her cloud of fine red hair, the odd flatness of her blue eyes which was like the surface of water, or like a mirror.

He watched her hands as she signed to the boy. She used a strange sign, touching her own body a great deal, and the face and hands of the boy, and of course there was no telling what any of that meant.

Each time someone passed on the sidewalks, blocking out the sight of her, he was afraid that when he looked again she would be gone.

After a moment he came to a decision. He went into the back room and rolled the fox pelt into a bundle and tied it with a thong. He took from the wall a small dusty squaw-doll that had hung there on a nail for years, and slipped this under the thong.

The girl and the child were still on the bench when he went out. He laid his hand on the back of the girl's head and placed the bundle on her lap. The boy leaned near her and they studied the Indian doll together, and then the boy looked up and said, "Are you giving it to her?"

Carl went around and knelt in front of the girl and untied the thong.

Open it, he signed, but the girl shook her head.

He opened the pelt and spread it across her knees. He laid the doll in the center of it.

You can keep this, he signed.

The girl shook her head, again, and Carl lifted the small arms of the doll where it lay in the fur, so that it looked as though it was reaching for the girl. The small plaster face was vivid, with its red cheeks and black eyes.

Don't you want the doll? he signed.

When the girl shook her head the third time, he rolled the fur up roughly with the doll inside of it, and tied it with the thong.

You are a child, he signed to her angrily.

She sat motionless, looking away to the side. He threw the pelt across the sidewalk and through the doorway of his store.

I speak to you, he signed. *Who else can I speak to? Grow up a little bit. Use your head.* He tapped his forehead angrily.

The girl pushed a strand of hair behind her ear, and Carl saw in this gesture how much she dreaded him. He realized then that she would never speak to him, and in that moment a memory came to him of a time in his youth when he had tried to swim across a broad, nearly frozen lake in the mountains near the border of France. His strength had given out somewhere in the middle, and two fishermen not far off had had to come after him in their boat. He remembered their faces, grim and silent, as they leaned over to take hold of him.

He saw, in the delicate curves under the girl's eyes, a fine sheen of perspiration.

He got up and went back into the store.

He stood in the center of the room with his back to the door, thinking – I will close early today. I will work on the car, find out where the oil is leaking. After that I will take the grape slips, that have stayed already too long in the bucket, and plant them at the foot of the garden.

He ran his hand through his hair, and watched the wind from the open door slip into a pile of red and orange silk scarves that he'd laid out on the counter. Then he felt the girl's hand on his arm, and he turned.

Do you know the swallows? she signed to him.

Say again?

Swallows. In that place by the river.

I care nothing about that, he signed.

He picked up the fox pelt from the floor, and put it under her arm, and made her hold it there.

You want to come? she signed.

Come? Where?

Come now.

A feeling he had not known in years, a feeling he had forgotten about, overcame him then, and in his confusion he took his watch out of his pocket and looked at it, but she covered it with her hand.

Come, she signed. *Come now.*

The green truck traveled fast. The sky lay flat and brilliant on its windows. The evening light froze the old road into a long piece of silver with dust on it. Along the roadside, dew had already gathered on the cactus and had set the spider webs to glittering everywhere over the stony ground.

Carl was surprised by the way the girl drove the truck. She drove a little too fast, working the gears skillfully. He observed that she could drive a pick-up easily, and he noticed also how good she was with the boy. He no longer thought of her as a child. She was not a child. She was like the older children he had known in Germany during the war. The kind of child, he, himself, had been. Growing up in the space of a year, a few months.

The boy sat between them with a Bible open in his lap.

He had a mason jar full of sauerkraut juice clasped between his knees, and was eating a fried cake spread with honey. He put down the cake and held the Bible up with his finger on a passage which he wanted Carl to read. Carl looked closely at the place and read: "Thy teeth are like a flock of sheep. Thy two breasts are like young roes that are twins, which feed among the lilies."

The boy put his finger on the word, "roes," and signed, *Give meaning.*

Swans, Carl signed back to him.

Big birds?

Yes.

They eat lilies?

Yes.

The boy finished his fried cake, thinking about this, and licked his fingers.

And teeth like sheep? he signed.

It's after they're shorn, Carl signed, *and they line up hungry at the fence.*

When they had left the town behind by several miles, Carl rolled down the window and rested his elbows on the sill. It had been a long time since he had come out into the countryside. Bands of sheep at the fence sped by quickly, and beyond them began the endless stretches of cactus and thorny mesquite. Carl looked across the sweep of the land, which glowed with a tired, tallow-colored light, and watched the foreshortened sun sinking into a haze of dust at the horizon.

They turned off the highway onto a dirt road, and the girl pointed out a string of birds, a shifting dark line converging on the sun. This reminded him of the story about the boy with wings who flew too close to the sun, and then he thought about what it felt like to swing a heavy gun against his shoulder, and swiftly fire, and watch, out of a line like that one near the horizon, one bird finally, miraculously, fall.

They passed the reservoir, and he looked up at the long edge of the dam. He saw a solitary man silhouetted there with his arms raised as though in praise of the water, which

72

lay rare and vast at his feet, or of the sky which was filled with a kind of candlelight at that hour, or of the earth which was turning slowly towards the darkness.

Having finished his meal, the boy lay down with his head in the girl's lap. The girl's eyes were narrowed against the sun, which lay directly ahead of them, and she seemed deeply contented to be driving at that hour and in that direction.

A few miles further on, they crossed over a plank bridge, and Carl caught sight of an old sycamore tree rooted in the shallow bank of the river. Not far beyond that, the girl pulled off the road in front of a barn and stopped the motor. They sat, motionless, looking at the barn. It was a huge barn. An old German barn. The kind Carl had played in at his grandfather's farm in the years before the war. He knew of a German settlement many miles to the south where there were warm valleys with vineyards, but there were no Germans here. He couldn't understand how such a barn could be there.

Who owns this barn? he signed to the girl.

I do, she answered him.

You own this barn?

She glanced at him and laughed. *Nobody owns anything,* she signed.

The boy raised up, sleepily, and the girl opened the door and got down out of the truck.

The swallows are flying, she signed.

Carl watched the swallows circling the barn, following each other in and out through gaps in the walls. Then he saw the long shadow that the barn made on the ground, and it occurred to him that it was very late in the evening.

How long are we staying here? he asked the girl, but she was walking away and couldn't see him, so he got down out of the truck and caught up with her and turned her towards him.

How long do you want to stay here? he signed.

Are you hungry? she signed. *I have food.*

73

It's late, and we have no light.

It isn't dark.

We've come very far out.

Far? she signed. *Far from what?* She took his hand and pulled him with her through the big doors.

The interior of the barn had a dappled, sheltered feeling that was like being underwater. The girl stood close to him and signed something to him. He took her hands and pressed the palm of one to his lips. She frowned and pulled away and tried to sign again, but he caught her and held her against him. The swallows flew near, calling, and the evening sun struck sharply through the walls, streaking the floor and lighting up the girl's hair. He felt the quickened beat of her heart. The smell of her was like alfalfa brought in fresh from the threshing. She put her hands on his waist. Holding her, he felt himself beginning to rest deep in his spirit after a desire of so many years.

They left the boy playing in the barn and walked down to the river. The river was a small black stream about as wide as a woman's waist. It slipped darkly through the center of its bleached limestone bed. They went at first right up to the water. The girl showed him how fine the water was to drink, as if this was something only she knew about.

The sun had dropped out of sight, leaving behind it along the horizon a hazy legion of thunderheads lit around the edges with fine gold wires.

It was the time of evening when the swallows converged on the river. They swooped in long curved flights, feeding on the clouds of gnats hovering low over the warm stones.

Carl and the girl climbed to a ledge of limestone under the sycamore tree. He took his comb out of the pocket of his shirt and made her sit with her back to him so he could comb out her hair. Her red hair was full of gatherings of fine curls which at first he didn't want to disturb but desired, instead, to press gently between his fingers the way one might press the paws of a small drowsy animal. She sat with her head bent slightly and her hands folded in her lap, wearing an air of seriousness and obedience in which he perceived, somewhere far back in her childhood, the tending of a woman. He combed her hair out in waves over his arm the way he'd seen his mother do every morning with his younger sister. When it was all combed through, he twisted the mass of it up onto her head, and ran a finger along the small knobs of her spine.

She took the comb from him and parted his hair in the middle. She combed his hair to the sides and licked her fingers to wet it down. Then she hid the comb away from him in the folds of her dress, laughing, and turned and settled herself back into the curve of his body. He took her hands in his own. Her legs swung free over the edge of the limestone. He was greatly comforted by the slow swinging of her dusty feet and by the feel of her sturdy body. He wondered how soon the night would come, and what it would be like. He knew it would be vast, and that the mantle of stars would overwhelm him, but for now he was deep into a feeling that was as elusive and pure as the dark ribbon of water in the riverbed, and nothing at this time could hold any fear for him.

They spent the night in the topmost loft. The girl slept heavily with her head on Carl's arm, and once he brushed her hair back from her cheek and felt the dampness underneath. The boy slept curled at their feet.

Carl looked up through the gaps in the roof and watched the stars journeying. The moon slid like a kite before him with small rags of clouds crossing it. He thought of the old magnolia tree which grew in his yard and which seemed, at night, always to be moving in one direction while the stars and clouds moved in another. He thought of his garden and of the vine with blue flowers he had trained along the fence. His yard would be bright like a lake in the moonlight now, and the garden would be a disturbance in it, like a monster surfacing. He thought of his bed under the open window, the sheets tangled and thrown back. He thought of his leather slippers side by side on the mat.

Once the girl started violently in her sleep. He put his arm over her, across her breasts, to protect her.

He was dreaming of the village where they sent him as a boy during the war. He knew he was lying in the barn in the early morning with the girl asleep against his side, but the dream moved in closer and enfolded him and he found himself in a field of poppies in which he was running with the other children. Across the canal, many women were bending low in a stubble field, binding armfuls of barley. Near them was a plot of big vines with melons swelling under the leaves. He would love to take one of those melons if he could get across, he thought, and so he stood at the edge of the water, beating two sticks together to get the women's attention. When they turned to him, he tightened his arms around the girl and signed, *Show me the way across.* The nearest woman smiled and motioned for him to come forward, and he waded into the water, holding the girl tightly so she wouldn't be swept away from him by the current. She struggled to free herself from him, but he pressed his lips to her forehead and lifted her higher and began to swim. As he swam, he held the girl steady with his arms and legs, protecting her, and the cold stream closed over them, and he thought soon they would be across, but the water was very wide. He peered upward through the dark water, trying to see the women and the green vines with their melons, but all he could make out was the dappled surface towards which he was rising. The girl struggled more powerfully against him. He held onto her with all his strength, but she broke loose, finally, and was carried away. The bright surface of the water shattered over him, then, and he woke at the edge of the loft looking down into a great many motes of light with chaff drifting through them. The girl lay far below on the floor. He turned and saw the boy backing away under the eaves, crying.

He looked through the wide baling window and caught sight of the swallows gliding swiftly like a cloth over the distant trees. The cloth lifted and sank, catching the sun like mail, then disappeared behind the sycamore by the river.

William Henry followed a short distance behind the deaf man. The man was carrying Angel to the river. William Henry wanted to run in front of him and sign to him to go back, but he was afraid; he could tell, anyway, from the look on the man's face, that nothing would stop him.

There was no wind, and the air was like a piece of hot, brittle paper about to burn. William Henry wished that he had taken the time to pull on his boots. It was hard to keep going barefooted over the rough ground.

When they reached the river, a wind with a sharp edge struck him, and he looked up and saw that the sky had turned deep green and was churning and moving swiftly. Along the horizon was a band of clear air active with lightning.

He stood on the bank, watching the deaf man carry Angel down into the riverbed. He felt the first big drops of rain come heavily, then, and dark spots appeared on the stones. The rain increased and soon the ground was darkened with it, and rivulets of water began running down the erosions into the river.

The deaf man laid Angel down at a place in the middle on a sheet of small pebbles. His shirt was plastered to his back with rain. Angel's hair clung wetly to her face. He put her beside the narrow stream of water, straightening her legs and arranging her dress, and then continued on across the river to the other side.

After that the man stood on one bank and William Henry stood on the other, and they watched the rain sweeping by between them in heavy sheets.

Close by William Henry, the sycamore was flattened back by the force of the storm. Soon he sat down beside it with his knees drawn up, holding his feet in his hands, full of the fear of being blown away. On the other side of the river, the deaf man stood with his head down, his back to the wind.

When Angel was lifted and carried away by the flood-water, William Henry followed her along the bank of the river. He stumbled down the shallow ravines and up the cliffs and went running along the narrow shale beaches, trying to keep her in sight.

She was carried lightly, floating on the crests of the swells. The river had turned her around and now bore her head first, as if with intent, as if there was a certain way such a journey was taken, and Angel was secure, now, with the river, and would travel well and safely through all that lay ahead.

William Henry followed her as far as he could, but she was being carried, and he was running on his own. He came to a place where the water slid into sheer walls of limestone like a tunnel with light in it. He was confronted there by a towering shoulder of rock. He made a sudden decision to sit in the shelter of it.

The wind had died away. The rain continued coming straight down, heavily. The river, which was traveling almost silently, with no turbulence, carried with it sheets of white froth which separated and reunited languidly over the speeding surface.

The people had come to the park by the river because it was cool, now, after the rain, and they wanted to sit at the low tables under the oak trees, in the presence of heavy and abundant water, and eat their chicken and boiled eggs and whole fresh tomatoes held in the hand like a peach.

The grown-ups stayed at the tables, talking and holding the babies until way into the evening, when the sun, having descended slowly through the vistas of red and purple that follow upon a storm, touched the horizon and diminished to the flame of a candle.

A child ran up from the river, calling, "Father, you've got to come. Please. Everybody. Everybody come."

All the men and two of the women with babies in their arms got up and followed the child. The other women stayed at the table, clearing away the food while they talked, folding wax paper over the bowls, and carrying the paper plates to the barrel.

The child took her father's hand and led him out to a narrow beach in the river. The other men followed behind, and then the women, and the bank of the river struck a shadow over them as they descended down to the water's edge. All the children, even the very small ones, were gathered on the rough shale beach, and all were very quiet and still, standing around something which they were looking at together.

The child brought her father into the crowd of children and commanded everyone to move back.

"Let my father see," she said.

The father came into the group, and looked down with the others.

"See?" the child said. "See there? What did I tell you?"

The other men came up and looked down, and then the women, and everybody was quiet for a long time.

Finally, one of the women said, "You'd think she was smiling. Look at her face."

"She's alive," said one of the children.

"No. Not that one," a man said.

"Yes," the child said.

Looking for Rain

The grandfather sat on the steps watching as the old mud-colored Mercury paused at the gate and then turned slowly onto the rutted country road. Through the chimera of heat, the old man could see the top of the car as it moved down the road on the other side of the stone wall. The car slammed with a jouncing, bottom-scraping sound over the ruts, and the two people in the front seat bounced back and forth wildly like people in a carnival ride. He pictured the old car finally giving way under this rough usage, disintegrating with one horrific slam into a jumble of scrap metal all over the road, and the two people tossed and upended in the ditch with their necks broken. But nothing of that sort happened, of course, and soon they were out of sight, leaving him there just like they'd intended, alone with the child.

"Granddaddy, I don't believe it's altogether that much to ask," Carla Sue had told him earlier that morning. "Not once in this great while."

But that wasn't the point, and he'd told her so. The point was the nature and disposition of the child in question. A six-year-old, straggle-haired, skinny-legged brat, big as a wildcat now, with the same inclination to leap out of nowhere when you weren't looking and sink her teeth into you.

"But I've told her strictly she's not to do that anymore," Carla Sue had said. "If she uses her teeth the least little bit, you let me know, hear?"

The grandfather stared darkly down the path at the little wilted stand of chinaberry trees that ranged along the barbed-wire fence. If she used her teeth the least little bit he'd snap a few bones in her neck. He'd had about all he could take of those two young people spoiling their only child rotten, never asking for nor caring about advice from someone who'd raised five of his own and might have something to say on the subject. By God, look at the pass they'd come to—

a solitary child ruling everything and everybody with her tantrums and her whims, using her teeth, even, if anybody dared to cross her. He'd never in his days seen a child to match her.

Well, he wouldn't have asked to be put in charge of her, no way would he have asked it, but now that he was he had a feeling that there was going to be a change in the wind. He had a feeling that there was going to be something that that child had never yet heard of – something she needed like the prairie out there needed rain – descend on her sure enough in the next few hours.

Where was she, anyway? Carla Sue had given her cloth and scissors for cutting out patches on the kitchen floor, then sneaked out to the gate where Willy waited with the car. But the trick was bound to have worn off by now. Nothing could hold that child for long.

He rubbed his palms on his knees, feeling the sweat roll down inside his shirt. The back of his head began prickling. He had the feeling that she was standing behind the screen-door with the scissors in hand, looking out at him, but he was damned if he'd turn around to see.

At that moment there was a pounding of feet inside and the screen-door flew open and slammed against the house. The grandfather jumped to the side as if he'd been struck and a tow-headed child streaked past him and out into the yard. She threw back her head and yelled, "Mama!" then picked up a stout stick and began beating the ground with it.

The grandfather stood and started backwards up the steps, steadying himself with a hand on the porch railing. He felt the goose-bumps rising up all over him. Great God, how did she know so soon that they was gone?

The child beat the ground until the stick, big around as a man's wrist, broke in two, then threw the stub away from her and stood swaying slightly, making a long, high sound in her throat.

He thought about going inside the house. He wanted to lie down on his bed with the door to his room locked and the shades pulled. He longed suddenly to let the child fend for herself if that was at all possible. Then he pictured himself locked in his room the whole day long, going without food, going without his walk down to Jagger's at the crossing, without the game of dominoes, without Jagger's good devil-eye whiskey and the glow it cast over the tail end of the day. He began to tremble while a cold fear swept through him. No matter how old you were nor how young you were you could never trust anyone to look after you. Old people and children were at the mercy of everything evil; and more often than not, it now seemed to him, they were at the mercy of it together.

The child turned, finally, and caught sight of him on the porch. Her face turned pale and calm in an instant and she reached up, like someone acting out something in her sleep, and slipped her fingers into the neck of her yellow dress. She pulled with all her strength until a button popped at the back, and then another, and then, suddenly, she was stretched out in the dusty yard going blue, her fists clenched at her throat and her legs jerking like a knocked-over hound's.

He stood it as long as he could, and then he climbed unsteadily down the steps and went and bent over her. He pushed at her hip with the toe of his boot, but he could see that the fit was as good a one as she'd ever had, and heaven nor earth was going to make her give it up. He squatted down and tried, with a trembling hand, to put her dress back into place where it had run down over her chest. Then, with a big, broad-nailed finger, he found the place he wanted high up beneath her breastbone, and began to press hard. After a moment, her eyes focused with the pain, and she gave a squeal and came alive fast. She folded like a jack-knife around his arm and sank her teeth into his shoulder.

The grandfather jumped up and began to run around the yard with the child still fastened to him. He was tilted to that side like a turkey with a broken wing. Cursing with fine abandon, he struggled up the steps of the house, and, using the porch railing, began to try to scrape the child off him in such a way that she would have a good fall into the iron-hard bed of parched petunias.

Still she hung on, biting, and he began to grow faint with the heat and the pain, and it seemed to him that he could feel his rage rising all the way up from his boots. He remembered, briefly, that his teeth were false just before he came down with them, hard, on her naked shoulder, taking a good deal more flesh into the bite than she had done. He bit down with all his strength, almost wild with joy at the justice of it, the fine equality of their mutual rage and punishment; and when she finally squealed and let go, he pulled her off with both hands and threw her triumphantly into a wicker chair.

She flattened herself against the back of the chair like a lynx. There was a high spot of color in each of her cheeks, and her pale, blue-crystal eyes were leveled on the middle button of his shirt.

Suddenly, she screamed, "Fat Bugger!" at a pitch high enough to make his ears buzz. He took a step back and turned his head cautiously to observe how Carla Sue had tied her clothesline around two of the porch posts. He reached up and began to untie one end of this rope, and while he was doing this the child bolted from the chair, but he tripped her and upended the chair over her and nudged it sideways to make a cage against the porch railing. He held the chair in place with one knee while he went on working on the rope with unsteady hands. The child deafened him with her screams and got both hands caught in the wicker, but he continued untying first one end and then the other of the rope, paying her no mind.

He felt his way through the dark cellar until he got to the row of baskets, and then he felt around inside each one until he found the turnips. They were little blue turnips with lavender roots, and they beat rutabagas all to hell for flavor. He'd pulled these turnips himself, and had thought on them every day since that time, but Carla Sue hadn't seemed to hit on cooking them. He hadn't ever made any special requests, not once since he'd come to this house. Now he climbed back up to the kitchen with the turnips rolled up in his shirttail and dumped them on the table. He had the bacon already frying, and the water in the black kettle was rolling at a good boil. He peeled the turnips and quartered them into a pile, then scooped the white chunks into the kettle. He wiped the knife on his pants, folded it and slipped it back into his pocket. He thought of the turnips mashed up in the blue bowl with bacon drippings and coarse salt from the crock. They'd take more than an hour to cook.

He sat down at the table, pulled out his knife and tobacco and shaved off a plug. Then he leaned back a little until the child on the porch became visible through a corner in the window. Rope looked snug enough. She was quiet, he'd give her that. Smart enough not to yell and scream now there wasn't any use in it.

He rolled the plug around on his tongue, considering. In all his life he'd never tied an animal out in the sun without water. After a moment he sighed deeply, returned the knife and tobacco to his pocket and got up.

She didn't look up when he came out. He carried her own special silver cup, brimming with water. He pushed the door open with his foot and let it slam behind him.

"No chance you'd drink outa anything else, is there?" he said. "No telling how many times I got to fill it."

He crouched down beside her and brought the cup to her lips. When she made no move to drink, he laid a finger under her chin. "Come on, now," he said. Sweat glinted in the smooth curves beneath her eyes. The rope had rubbed her collarbone raw where her dress was pulled down. Had he done that? By God, she'd fought and clawed so hard there hadn't been any help for it.

The child dropped her head, avoiding the cup, and he tossed the water angrily out into the yard. It made a little dark splash in the sod, rolling up muddy beads that bubbled and sank. A small spotted dog rose from the petunias and crossed to sniff at the puddle, then raised his head and stared out across the prairie.

The grandfather watched a far-away hawk gliding in a slow spiral. After a time he sat down beside the child. He pried loose a sliver of wood from the step and began break-ing it into little pieces that fell between his boots.

"By God, I've a good mind to go on down to Jagger's," he said. "Leave you here to think on it. Be roasted like a little pullet time I got back." He shifted his weight impatiently, leaned back on his elbows. "How come you to be so stub-born? Ain't like no child I ever seen nor heard of."

He ran his hand slowly across the top of his head, then gave her a quick glance. She was slumped against the post, looking as though there was no way to slip down any further. Her thin legs, pocked with mosquito bites, were sprawled wide, and a wing of coarse, biscuit-colored hair closed in on her face from one side. He noticed how thin she was. Didn't her mama ever feed her? He recalled that the child was never at the table when they had the evening meal. Always running outside somewhere with the bats and the insects.

A memory came to him of a time when the child had come rushing into the kitchen, red in the face — that give it to me right now look she had — the screen door clattering behind her. Carla Sue had turned from the sink with a pinched face.

"Where's the big knife?" the child had called out to her mother.

"Oh, Baby, you know I can't let you have no such thing as that."

"Give it here right now!"

He had been standing in the door to the front room, watch-ing the knife where it lay beside a cut-up chicken on the board. She could just barely reach it, but she snatched it.

"Oh, Honey, give it back. Give it back to Mama. Please little Sugar."

There was a chase around the table, and, the last time around, the child had grabbed a handful of cold beans from the pot and made for the door.

Afterwards, Carla Sue had leaned wearily on the door-frame for a long while, looking out. "What's she want it for, do you suppose?"

86

Now he turned and looked at the child full on, remembering. A knife in one hand and cold beans in the other, running off who knows where.

If I let her loose, she'll bust the place to pieces, he thought, and then he thought, by God, what kind of an old woman are you getting to be? She ain't but a tenth your weight— lookit how puny she is.

"Straighten up there, Laney," he said. "Lookit you. Dress half off you. Hair in your face. Sprawled like a heathen."

"Just look at you," he said again. He took her legs by both knees and set them straight together on the steps. "Straighten up there, now," he said. He propped her up against the porch post like a rag doll. Her chin was on her breast, and her hair had slid forward on both sides of her face, closing her off.

"Let's see here, now," he said, fumbling with a knot in the rope.

After a minute he loosened her hands and pulled the rope from her, hand over hand. She jerked with the pull of it, but other than that she had made no move. He regarded her carefully. She sat there as full of pep as a wrung-out mop. He felt the goose bumps rising again. It wasn't anyway natural the way she was sitting there. He pulled her up straight by one arm, took her by the jaw-bone and faced her out over the prairie.

"Lookit out yonder," he said. "Lookit out there way far off. See that there hawk? Well, that ain't no hawk. Just showed hisself to be a buzzard. Know what's under him? Jagger's new calf, that's what. Stillborn on the prairie in the wee hours. Betcha five dollars."

The child shied away from his hand and moved over a little, keeping her head down. She wrapped her arms around her knees and began rocking, a small, almost imperceptible motion.

"See there?" the grandfather said. "There's two more come to join him. What'd I tell you?"

The spotted dog came up the steps to thrust himself between the child's legs, and she crossed her wrists over his neck, frowning, dodging his tongue. The grandfather worked his mouth urgently for a moment, then spit a long brown stream sideways into the petunias and wiped his lips with the back of his hand.

He looked over beyond the outbuildings to the west where the prairie appeared to merge with the sky in a faint, sand-colored haze. There, rising above the darkening vague horizon, was a wide-spreading column of thunderheads, faraway but glorious.

"Guess we'll be looking for rain," the old man said.

Far out by the fence, the chinaberry trees stirred slightly in a fresh wind, the first over the prairie in several weeks. This meant rain tonight, or maybe tomorrow. Maybe only an hour of rain, maybe two, but the big drops would plop down, rolling up muddy beads in the dusty sod, and then the sky would open with a wall of water, and the prairie would soak and drink and run little rivulets off itself in every direction. The old house and the little slant-faced barn would steam and sigh under their streaming eaves. And afterwards, everything would cool off that little bit, and the prairie would green up almost overnight, a true summer green all around them for a while.

It took him half an hour to find a safety pin. The one he found, finally, way back in the kitchen drawer, was big enough to hang a steer from, but it would have to do.

He took the .22 down off the rack and cracked it open. Clean enough, probably. He spent more time cleaning these confounded guns than he did hunting with them. He stuffed the cartridges in his vest pocket and went out the front door.

The child sat hunched on the bottom step. Through the open back of her dress, the shiny white knobs of her backbone were visible the whole way down, and at the bottom was a little gray scrap of panties. She seemed to be made up entirely of a big straw hat and two black boots without laces sticking out at both sides. He propped the gun against

88

the porch and hauled her to her feet. Limp as a rag she was, still, with her head down, closing him out. One minute she was tearing your flesh from the bone, and the next minute she didn't have no more spunk than a mouse with its neck broke. Strange little number. He shoved her hat down tighter on her head and turned her around. He fastened the neck of her dress together with the safety pin, but there was still a three-inch gap the whole way down the back. What a sight. Tattered old hat, nothing but a rag of a dress, and those boots.

"Listen here," he said. "Ain't you got no shoes with laces in them?"

The big hat moved a little side to side.

"Let's get going, then," he said. "But listen here to me. Moment I got to pick you up and carry you, we're coming back."

She lifted her head and surprised him with a long look. Her lips were pressed together and her jaw was set in a line of pure hate. She looked him straight in the eye and he almost stepped back with the heat of it.

"God Almighty," he said. He picked up the gun. "I'm going," he said. "You can do as you please."

They crossed the prairie like two people that only happen by coincidence to be traveling the same way. Once or twice he looked back to see her stumbling over the rough terrain, charging red-faced through brush nearly as tall as she was.

When they got within sight of the prairie-dog town, a wide, bare crown of earth, stubbled with egg-sized stones, he slipped behind a heave of low rock and waved his hand urgently for her to get down. All she did was wander a little off to the side and come to a standstill, scuffing the dirt with one boot. He looked across and saw two prairie dogs melt away, with four or five more alerted, rearing up at the edge of their holes. What was they, up wind or down? God Almighty, what a no-account way to hunt. Big flapping calf of a child standing there in full sight of everything on the prairie.

89

He sighted on the white breast patch of the prairie dog turned fullest towards him. The shot cracked and echoed once, like another gun going off at the same time high up in the clouds. The dog jerked once and tumbled into a heap at the base of the mound.

The old man walked slowly over the stony ground and regarded the dead animal. Should have tried for a head shot, he thought. I've ruint half the meat.

He picked up the prairie dog by the hind feet and crossed towards the child, reloading his gun on the way. She began to back away as he approached. She had a pale, flat look on her face, and it occurred to him then that maybe she hadn't ever seen anything shot before. He beamed down on her and threw back his shoulders. With the fresh game and the gun in his hand he felt suddenly, surprisingly young. When had old age got to him? Crept up on him when he wasn't looking. Seems he'd bought the whole bill of goods without realizing what he was doing.

He gazed down at the child and was again amazed at how puny she was. Looked like she might be in for a case of the shakes. He took her roughly by the shoulders and forced her down. "Set!" he said, and he sat down himself on a stone in front of her. "I'm going after hare, now," he told her, "and I don't want no company." He took out his knife, rolled the prairie dog over in his lap, and made a slit in both hind feet. The child's eyes grew large, watching while he threaded a stick through the feet and hung the game on his belt. "These here prairie dogs'll lie low for a spell," he said. "But after a bit they'll come out to see what's what. If you kin sit here without moving a hair 'til I get back, maybe we'll stand a chance on getting us another one." He stood and sighted down the gun in a long swing, following a blackbird, then cradled the gun in his arms. "Not that there's much hope of that," he said looking down at her.

He had covered about ten yards when a stone sailed past him, so close to his head that he started at the whistle of it. He whirled about, bellowing, "Christ Almighty!" and caught another full in the chest. This caused him to drop his gun and stagger sideways and a big pinwheel of fire began to turn in his frame, and he had a vision of his heart at the center of it, stunned and motionless. White comets of light sought to burn out his vision, but in between them he perceived the child bending over prying loose another stone from the ground. She looked like a flapping, knobby-kneed doll that someone had fashioned with the poorest workmanship, and he began to laugh along with her the way you do some no-account midget in the circus. He stumbled forward, reaching out, but just before he got hold of her, a stone turned under his foot. He saw her look of astonishment, saw her arms come up to catch him, as the wide plane of earth turned swiftly, rising like a wall, and smote him full in the face before there was time to let out his in-drawn breath and yell.

He woke to a strong, hot wind blowing over him, and the rumble of thunder. He knew in an instant where he was and what had happened, and he heard someone whisper hoarsely in his ear, "Could be she's kilt me," and then realized it was his own voice. He turned his head first to one side and then the other and saw death approaching him from all directions over the prairie, rolling up in a heavy green vapor through the prickle bush low to the ground.

He felt as though he were coated with a skin of mud that had dried and cracked in the sun, and it came to him that he had fallen directly onto an antbed and the ants had crawled in through every crack and set to stinging him all over. He frowned and prepared a fine stream of curses but then fell to coughing in a long fit that he thought would never stop.

He was certain that he had been awakened to be given advantage of those few minutes that he had played through many times in his mind. For years he had been perfectly certain that in his final moments he would be given a glimpse into the unknown of death that would make it less fearful. He had pictured a large hand stretched out to him and a voice echoing as though through endless chambers, crying, "Abraham Stone, you were right about it. Heaven is a familiar country, in no way to be feared." Yet now, when he looked within, everything was as dark as it had always been, and all he heard was a multitude of slithering sounds that might be the brush twigs rubbing together, or something else entirely.

He felt a shadow cross him then, and, looking straight up, perceived that the three buzzards, done with Jagger's calf, had come to circle over him. He rolled over, yelling, "Not as long as I got any breath left in me!" and heaved himself upright on his knees. Immediately something leaped at him from the side, causing him to bellow and shy away as though bitten. The thing clung to him and he beat at it with both hands before he realized that it was the prairie dog attached to his belt. He sank down, weak in the joints, gazing at the sweat from his face as it dropped down in the dust.

He looked out over the merciless, forever-looking stretches of pricklebush and cactus and began to shake all over, trying to remember how far out they'd come from the house. The landscape looked utterly foreign to him, and the two years that he'd inhabited it fell away from him, and he began to curse himself for having come so far away from the sun-flickered clearings and the cool, hushed expanses of his piney-woods. God, look at how he'd betrayed himself, seeking cover like a yellow cur-dog with his no-account granddaughter and her shiftless husband in this hell-hole of a country. He remembered striding proud over the board-walks at the mill where he had been saw-boss for so many years, and the niggers, with their log poles, hurrying off around the banks of the pond, saying, "Yessir, Mr. Stone, we get these here timbers set straight in no time." And once again he reached up and pulled on the rope, giving the long whistle-blast that shut down the saws at closing time.

Then he felt the blood rise up full in his face with shame. For here he was, an old man on his knees, struck down by a piddling child, pulling for all he was worth on an invisible rope in the middle of this God-forsaken prairie.

He staggered to his feet and began to walk unsteadily towards the low hills that beckoned him, blue and gentle, in the distance. Then out of the corner of his eye he caught a quick movement nearby. He looked over and there was the prairie-dog town, with a half dozen members of the population reared up at the edge of their holes, staring at him as though he was some lunatic stumbled into town, cracked-lipped and crazed from the sun.

He bent down then to pick up the gun, and when he straightened up again the landscape shifted subtly – a swift, dizzying, almost imperceptible motion – and fell into place around him.

There, a half mile down the long slope, was the stand of chinaberry trees, and behind that, the familiar house and barn set on their ribbon of straggly green alongside the dried-up, rubble-bedded creek.

Many hours later he woke in his own room in the deep of night. His head ached dully and felt like it was several inches too thick on one side. He became aware of the house asleep around him. He recalled Carla Sue coming to his door to ask after the child, and, later, coming again to inquire if he was up to coming to the table. He had given her no answer. He had lain there, under the light coverlet, exhausted, all through the evening hours, dwelling on the peace of the growing darkness and the softness of his bed.

Now, suddenly, in the deep night, a stark white rectangle flashed once and then again before his eyes, and three heavy seconds later there came a dull, far-rolling crack of thunder. The roar that had been in his head for some time located itself then as the steady, ponderous sound of the rain outdoors.

In that moment, he became aware of a weight on his legs, and it came to him that he'd had a stroke while he was sleeping and was now paralyzed, probably, from the waist down. Then the lightning flashed again, illuminating the whole room briefly, and he caught sight of the child sitting cross-legged on top of him, staring at his face with dark, shining eyes.

"Damn," he said, and the word lay softly in the air, and the next time the lightning flashed, the child was still sitting there looking at him with the same expression.

He reached down and pulled on the covers, but they merely grew taut under the child's weight and barely reached to his waist. He shifted his legs out from under her and started to sit up, but she climbed with sharp-jabbing knees straight up his body and weighted him down by the shoulders while the lightning flashed again in her eyes only inches from his own.

"You been listening to it, too?" she whispered in the darkness.

"What in thunder?" he said, croaking out the words, unable to breathe under her weight.

"That's right," she said. "I thought so. You cain't sleep for it neither."

Then she shoved his arm away from his body and flopped over and curled up into a ball against his ribs.

He lay there rigid, preparing in every limb to leap from the bed, but after a long moment all she said was, "Ain't you going to pull up the covers?" When he still didn't move, she reached down and pulled the covers up herself and tucked them patiently around him, like an old woman with a very young child. Then she settled down underneath until all that was left sticking out was the top of her head.

A little while later, lying on his side with his back towards her, he whispered, "God Almighty! Ain't you got nothing but knees on your body?"

But she only nudged all her little sharp knobs deeper into his back, and he felt the warm small cloud of her breath, like a cat's, low down on the back of his neck. Outside, the rain poured on with such abandon that he began to imagine that they were afloat on a vast ocean, small but well-kept in the darkness, while the storm rolled restlessly on, already forgetting them, already passing on to some other corner of the earth.

The Bath

R oy Junior's mother always asked him to go outside whenever she bathed his grandmother. This happened every
day all through the summer. In late afternoon, when his
grandmother needed cooling off, his mother would carry a
basin of water, a fresh towel and washrag, and a bar of Life-
buoy soap into the front room where his grandmother lay
taking up hardly any space at all in her rickety iron bed.
When his mother set the basin of water down on the table,
she would call out at the top of her lungs, "Roy Junior, it's
Mamaw's bath time now, honey." Then, wherever he was
in the house, he would know that it was time for him to step
outside for a while.

Usually he hauled his bike off the porch and coasted down
the long, shallow grade to the store, just to see what was
happening; but today the thought of this brought with it a
wash of weariness. What would he see, anyway, that hadn't
already impressed itself on him a hundred thousand times?
The ditch alongside the road, full of dry weeds. The few
houses on the one side, the church on the other. And the
store. With its old Coca-Cola sign tacked across the rusty
screen door, its flies, its smell of kerosene and beer.

So instead of going to the store, he sat down on the front
porch steps. He picked up a large flake of mud with straw
in it and began crumbling this idly between his feet. His
black hair grew low on his forehead; his hands were large
and red. His eyes appeared always to carry the same question in them.

He had worked all that morning, as he did every morning
through the summer, moving cattle in the stockyards across
the railroad tracks. He had come home at noon, weak
through the hips from hours on the back of a stiff-gaited
pony; he had sat on the edge of his bed slowly removing his

boots, his chaps, his sweat-stiffed pants. Now he wore a brown tee shirt with a picture of a long-legged bird taking flight across the front of it and a pair of cut-off jeans.

He gazed out across the highway at the flat, endless stretches of mesquite, and began to think about his father. He remembered sitting here on the porch many times with his father. He remembered the dust on his father's boots, the thin brown whiskey bottle in the pocket of his jacket. As they sat on the porch in the evenings, with the town growing dark around them, his father would roll himself a brown, twisted cigarette, and light it delicately, cupped between his palms. Through the slow-drifting smoke of this cigarette, they would gaze together for long periods over the darkening stretches of prickly-pear cactus and low mesquite spreading without end before them. Roy Junior would catch, in these silences, a glimpse of his father's other life. As far back as he could remember, his father had always been off somewhere, breaking into some new line of work in different parts of the country. The last time he'd come to visit them was four years ago.

Roy Junior pulled his shirt off over his head and dried his face with it. While his mother bathed his father's mother in the front room behind him, he took a harmonica out of his back pocket and began to play. Through the open window, he heard the two women speaking together. They spoke about something that had happened several years ago. An elderly neighbor woman had come to the house and accused his grandmother of stealing a large family Bible out of her living room. His grandmother had had to defend herself against this accusation for several weeks, until finally one day the woman came over to apologize, saying that her daughter had borrowed the Bible and forgot to mention it. This incident had become one of the things his grandmother was always remembering though she never recalled the part about the Bible being found.

"It doesn't matter any more, Clara," Roy Junior heard his mother say.

"I have said it and said it, but it's only my word," replied his grandmother in a voice like the weeds rustling together beside the porch.

"Hush, now. It's all gone by."

"Lord God, before heaven!"

"It's nothing, only an old memory always coming around."

"But she's going to come here again today."

"Hush. She was here already. I shooed her off."

Roy Junior, listening to the women's voices over the sound of the harmonica, was remembering the long, anxious months of the winter and spring when his mother hadn't had a moment's peace worrying that his grandmother would kill herself suddenly with the impossible things she was always taking on. He remembered his mother saying to him one day, "Don't you go down and buy her any flower seeds."

"She is going to die of feeling useless, then," he said.

They had looked together out the window at his grandmother standing by the gate with the rake in her hand, looking first one way down the road, then the other.

"It's going to get worse until she gets the seeds," he had said.

"It was always her spoiling you, only now it's the other way around," his mother said. She was a large woman with mockery in her eyes and a voice as deep, nearly, as a man's. Her heavy hair was always sagging down out of its tortoise-shell pins.

As it turned out, his grandmother had found some seeds on her own, in a matchbox far back in a drawer. She had scraped at the hard-packed earth in the front yard with the rake, dropping the seeds one by one into the shallow grooves, packing them down with loud, dusty slaps of her foot. Roy Junior sat on the porch steps watching, until he couldn't stand it any longer, then he called out, "Mamaw, you can't just put seeds in the bare *ground.*" But she went on packing the seeds down, dragging the rake along behind her.

Now almost the whole yard, on both sides of the path, was

covered with the stand of firebushes that had come from those seeds.

The women's voices, continuing beneath the surface of his awareness, expanded the space around him like the action of yeast in bread. As far out over the range as he could see, the undulating masses of heat contorted everything slightly, condensing, after a certain distance, into countless small burnished-silver lakes. Nearby a wasp droned angrily in the wood of the eaves.

A young woman with a child on her hip came out of the house next door. She stepped down from the porch onto a cinder block that was used as a step. Her name was Rosa Carmela, and Roy Junior was deeply in love with her. She had rose-honey tones in her brown skin, and her arms were rounded and smooth. She had tied her long, heavy braids together at the ends with a red rag. Much of the asbestos siding was missing from her house, with the tar paper showing underneath. Strings of red chilies hung on each side of the front door, and a brightly painted clay pot with a dead plant in it lay on its side beside the step. A small mimosa tree, covered with a cloud of pink blossoms, grew at the corner of the porch.

Rosa Carmela crossed with the child to a black truck that was parked out in the sun. She climbed in behind the wheel, leaving the door open, and laid the child back into the curve of her arm. Then she unbuttoned her blouse for him to nurse.

Roy Junior, hidden from her by the porch railing, blew softly into the harmonica, more breath than tone.

Jesus Miguel, Rosa Carmela's husband, came barefooted out of the house. He stood in the yard, a thick-set man with a dense mat of hair on his chest and arms, looking at his wife. Suddenly he rushed to the side of the truck and slammed the door closed, causing the child to scream in terror. Then he raised both hands clasped together and brought them down very hard on the roof of the truck.

Rosa Carmela, weeping loudly, climbed out the other side,

98

still holding the child. She hurried towards the door of the house, but her husband caught her by her wrists. He forced her to her knees and the child fell to the ground. Then Jesus Miguel got into the truck. He backed it onto the road in a cloud of dust and drove away.

When the truck was finally out of sight, Roy Junior found himself standing at the bottom of the steps. While he hesitated there, Rosa Carmela quieted the child and lay down with him under a wide-spreading chinaberry tree, which was the only shade in the yard. Roy Junior watched her for a long time without moving. Finally, he went slowly back up the steps and sat down.

When it seemed as though Rosa Carmela and her child might be asleep, he began to play again softly on his harmonica. Across the road a mockingbird began to answer him. The mockingbird sat on the announcement board in front of the church, which, for as long as he could remember, had read, "HAVE YE BATHED IN THE BLOOD OF THE LAMB?" Whatever Roy Junior played, the mockingbird tried to answer, picking up, roughly, the spirit of the music and a good bit of the cadence.

Roy Junior watched Rosa Carmela sleeping, curled up on her side with the child against her. He recalled, a few days earlier, seeing his grandmother sleeping in exactly the same position. He had gone into the house thinking that the bathtime was over. As he passed through the hallway, he had caught sight of his grandmother lying on her side with her knees drawn up, naked except for a white towel laid over her chest. His mother was nowhere in the room. He had a sudden desire to go in and look at his grandmother closely all over, especially her face and her hands, which had grown very frail and delicate. Instead, he went out the back door to a place far behind the house where an old green Mercury truck with the wheels missing sat rusting in a bank of sand. He had climbed into the truck and sat behind the wheel, thinking about all the times his father had said to him, "Next time, Roy, I'll take you along."

Now as he watched Rosa Carmela asleep under the tree, he remembered his grandmother curled up in her bed with only a towel laid over her chest. He remembered the stillness, with not even a fly buzzing, in the large, nearly empty room.

He heard the screen door open behind him, and his mother said in a low voice that didn't quite get through to him, "Roy, Mamaw's gone."

He started to turn around to ask what she had said, but right then he saw Rosa Carmela's little white dog come out from under the house next door with something in its mouth, and cross to where the woman and child were sleeping.

"Come here! Come here!" he called softly to the dog, because he didn't want the two of them wakened.

"Honey, did you hear me?" his mother said.

"Gone? Gone where?" he said.

"She's dead."

He turned and looked up at her. She was leaning against the doorframe. Her eyes were dark and strange in her face. "I didn't finish her bath," she said. "We was just in the middle of it, then suddenly she was gone."

She went back inside the house, and Roy Junior stood looking through the screen door into the dark hallway.

He heard a whine behind him and turned to see that the white dog had come up on the porch and laid at his feet a small jaw-bone with a few teeth still in it.

"Now, don't you go fooling around over there, you hear?" he said to the dog. Then he went on into the house and into his grandmother's room.

His mother was just throwing the water from the basin out the open window. She turned to him and said in an unsteady voice, "She has soiled her bed. I guess the first thing to do is for you to lift her up so I can change it."

His grandmother lay stretched out on the bed completely uncovered. He went up to her, and his mother stood on the other side and they looked at the old woman lying between them. Her skin was like a long, carefully crafted garment

100

of chamois. The hand with the wedding ring on it lay on her breast. Roy Junior's mother looked at him, and her voice when she spoke felt like it was coming from far away. He leaned over and slipped his arms under his grandmother and lifted her up against him. She folded easily into just the right place. She was naked against his chest, her skin against his, her head fallen lightly over on his shoulder. He caught a glimpse then for the briefest moment of her being very much younger. He lifted her higher and held her closer and stood with her beside the open window. When he looked out, he saw the tree next door with all the flowers on it.

"No way to reach your father," his mother said behind him. "It could be he won't ever even know."

He thought of his father, then, the way he had last seen him, riding away in high spirits with three other men in the car.

"He had it all worked out," he said, "but he didn't know anything about it. He didn't know anything at all," and when the bed was ready, his mother had to speak to him softly for a long time, and remember with him, together, many things about his grandmother before he would lay her down.

The Stone Angel

The Indian boy woke before dawn. He looked through the window, and through the silvery branches of the pear tree with its hard little half-grown pears and saw the edge of the moon and a few stars. In the other bed, the old man, sleeping, was a mountain under the tattered quilt. He wore a red handkerchief tied around his nearly bald head to protect him from the roaches, of which he was deathly afraid. His face, on which was stamped a great weight of sorrow, looked over large and exposed in the moonlight.

The boy sat on the edge of his bed holding his cat. The cat was black with a white face. It was a small cat that had been nursed up on a bottle so had never grown to full size. The boy's large hands almost covered it, with only the white face showing, turned upward, the eyes squinted shut.

After a while the light began to change. A fresh wind with a sharp edge to it came in at the window. The boy dropped the cat down, hauled on his pants, went into the kitchen. He ran water onto his head, then flung back his hair and combed it carefully in front of a fragment of mirror that he had propped up over the sink. Two shirts hung on the back of the door, one brown and shapeless, mended with several different colors of thread, and another made of dark-blue rayon cloth with a pattern of red flowers in it. The boy put on the one with the red flowers, tucked it into his jeans, and began to prepare the breakfast.

Soon he heard the bedsprings creak in the next room. He heard the old man relieve himself in the bucket. The boy had prepared a batter out of cornmeal and a little bacon drippings, and when he heard the old man moving around he spooned the batter into cakes in the hot skillet. While he was doing this, the white-faced cat came up to him with a sound that was like a question in the back of her throat. He lifted her onto his shoulder.

When the breakfast of sidemeat and cakes and black coffee was nearly ready, the old man came into the kitchen. He stood beside the table studying the plates and forks laid down on it. He wore a woolen undershirt that had turned, over the years, the color of his own flesh, and a pair of khaki pants with the braces hanging down. In his good days he had been the best oratory revivalist in the memory of the county. More than a few who had heard him as children were still afraid of him.

The boy brought the skillet to the table, lifted the cakes onto the plates. He put the skillet back on the stove and sat down and began to eat. The old man hadn't moved.

"You going over there again today?" he said.

"Yes," the boy said.

"I thought it was only niggers went to it," the old man said.

The boy didn't answer. He could see the old man was deep into something he had in his head, that it was one of those times it was no use to talk to him.

"Come to think on it, I guess you're dark enough," the old man said.

The boy pushed the old man's chair back from the table with his foot. "Eat," he said.

"I've been watching you for a long time being nose-led by the devil," the old man said.

"Yes?" the boy said. "How long is that?"

"How long? Overlong," said the old man. He had begun to breathe heavily.

"Sit down. Christ Almighty!" the boy said.

He got up, took a mug off the shelf and poured the old man some coffee. The old man tested his chair to see if it was steady, then sank down slowly into it.

"You sure don't waste time," the boy said.

The old man poured some of his coffee into a saucer. He blew on this for a minute, then looked up at the boy. "Yes, I waste time," he said. "I waste *my* time."

"I got something I want to do over there," said the boy.

"You want to go to the devil," the old man said.

The boy laughed. "How far could I go?" he said.

"You stay home," the old man said.

"What are you doing here, now," said the boy. "You going to give me trouble?"

The old man placed both hands on the table and rose ponderously, knocking his chair over.

"The Lord spread before me a vision of this whole abomination," he said. "At my right hand is the angel of fire."

"Christ," said the boy. "I am going to wash up after this breakfast, and then I am going over there."

The old man crossed to the door. He closed it and bolted it.

"You are going to give me trouble," said the boy.

The old man reached for the heavy buffalo gun he kept over the door, which they both knew had been neither cleaned nor loaded in all the time the boy had lived there. When he threw the bolt on this gun and turned back, the boy was gone.

The boy moved through the waist-high sorghum easily, taking two rows at a time in his long stride, leaving behind him a wake of silver in the green. The cat traveled ahead of him with a tight, quick gait. He caught sight now and then of her white face, looking back, waiting, moving on.

When they reached the edge of the planted field, they faced a long expanse of stony pasturage with many sheep on it. This sloped down into a broad valley with a town in the center of it, wedged into the bend of a silver river. Separated from the town by a half mile of low-growth mesquite, a cluster of tents and brightly painted trailers and rides looked out of place in the dull brown countryside. The ferris wheel, fragile as fine wire, was empty and ghostly at that hour of the morning.

The boy called to the cat, lifted her onto his shoulder. As they moved down the slope, the sheep ran a few feet away from them as they passed, then dropped their heads to pull jerkily on the tough dry grass.

The boy had been gone for two days. The old man opened the screen door slowly and went out on the porch. He stood at the edge of the steps looking down into the wide rose bed with a stepping stone path laid down in it that the boy had in the yard. The boy had positioned among the rosebushes all the pieces of carved stone he'd collected over the years, among them a lamb and a larger than life-sized hand with a ring on the little finger. A stone angel with wide-spread wings knelt, praying, in the center of the rose bed. She was about as high as a man's waist. The old man had threatened many times to crack her in two with an ax handle, believing her to have been taken from one of the spires of the Pope's church in Rome, Italy, which was the seat of the devil.

He watched the angel, waiting for some subtle movement that would betray her – a finger slipped into the wrong position, an eyelid lifted for a glimpse of him, a smile. It had become a habit with him, this watching the angel. As he watched her now he thought about the boy. He thought about that first day when the boy's mother, a skinny harlot with black hair pulled back into leather straps and both wrists covered with silver, had appeared on the path with the boy and an old woman. The old woman was bent over and wore a black ragged shawl around her shoulders. The boy held fast to her hand. The boy's mother had named the man – it was the old man's second son, with whom he'd lost all connection – who was the boy's father.

After that the boy had lived with the old man for ten years. He'd grown to be about six-and-a-half feet tall with a strength in him well known to everyone. He never talked to the old man about where he'd come from or why he was living there. Sometimes the old man worried about how much he could recall.

He thought about how clean and precise the boy was in his ways, about how he'd taken over the cooking and the care of the house the way a woman would. He thought about the strangeness in the boy that had gnawed at him from the beginning, giving him cause to wake sometimes in the night and go and bend over where the boy lay sleeping to see what might be read on his face. The boy's strangeness was that he was never afraid. Or sorrowful. Or angry. He accepted everything the way a yucca will sometimes sprout through asphalt, growing tall and bearing its white blossoms untroubled by what's around it. But for the old man it was a different story. For him fear gathered like wolves. Even in the shelter of the house there were rooms he couldn't enter, chattering insects landing on him in the night. Frequently, there was a particular sound that made him think something was circling the cabin. When he heard it, he would bolt both the doors and keep the boy in the house until nightfall. He was afraid, too, of being poisoned. Only food prepared by the boy was safe.

He descended one step and leaned forward, searching the path the boy used when he went on foot. It was the longest he'd ever been gone. The old man was uneasy when he went away for even a few hours. Whenever the boy took the truck and went into town for supplies, the old man would wait on the porch with his cane on his knees. He would keep his eye on a spot beyond the planted fields where the truck, returning home, would lift a signaling of dust. There was plenty for the boy to do at home, the old man thought. Seldom reason that he could see for him to leave. The old man had been made aware, deep in his bones, of the voraciousness of evil, and of the difference between the home side and the other side of the gate.

He looked quickly at the angel. She was the devil's deception. She was the cleverness with which he had chosen to move in on the house. She had to be carefully watched.

He backed onto the porch and sank down into the wicker chair. He sighed deeply, planted his boots firmly one beside the other, laid his cane across his knees. The hours of waiting settled down on him like a yoke.

The boy stood in the dust of the promenade for half an hour watching the two men. No one walked past him while

107

he stood there, and the two men never looked up. They had spread a piece of red silk on the ground between them and were playing dice. They sat to one side of a platform with a motorcycle on it. After a while, the dwarf laid his cards face-up, rattled the dice, and rolled them on the silk. Both men laughed when they saw the throw, and the other man, the motorcycle rider, tossed his cards carelessly onto the cloth and stretched out on the ground with his head against an engine that was covered with a piece of suede leather. The dwarf, who was dark-eyed and pleasing to look at, collected the deck. He placed it together with the dice in the center of the silk and tied this into a bundle. Then he went over and sat down astride the other man, facing his feet; he lifted one of the man's legs and set to work on the muscles in the thigh.

When the boy came up to them, the motorcycle rider was laughing at something the dwarf had said. He was a big tight-muscled man, with a scarred face and yellow hair combed forward into a roll. When he looked up and saw the boy standing beside them, he said to him, talking about the dwarf, "This here is one of them Greek poets they tell you about."

The dwarf craned his head around to look up at the boy. "My God, that's a big palooka," he said.

"I saw you ride yesterday," the boy said to the motorcycle rider. He was thinking about the things he had seen the man do the day before.

The motorcycle rider was still laughing. "This here is a Greek and a dwarf and a poet all rolled up together," he said. "Isn't anything like him anywhere else on the planet."

"Do we have something you want?" the dwarf said, looking keenly at the boy. His eyes were lit up with humor and something darker, like a candle looked at through a brown glass bottle.

"I think you're good," said the boy to the motorcycle rider. "I think you're real good."

"Hey, Stavros," the man said, "tell that poem to this young

feller here. He would like to hear it."

"He's only a baby," the dwarf said, still looking up at the boy.

"No," said the boy, "that would be fine."

"Sit down, then," the motorcycle rider said.

The boy sat on the ground beside them, slipping a hand inside his shirt to feel the cat who was asleep against his skin.

"Hey, who invited you," the dwarf said. He rolled onto the ground and came close. The boy was amazed that now they were the same height. The dwarf studied him for a moment, then recited something in another language.

"Come again?" the boy said.

"Life springs from the word, 'yes,'" the dwarf said. He touched the boy's face lightly. "He's only a baby," he said. Then he turned and went through the doorway behind the platform. After a minute they heard the sound of metal hitting against metal, as if the dwarf were trying to open a valve or a cap by striking it with a wrench.

"I saw you yesterday," the motorcycle rider said. He had his arms crossed behind his head. His eyes were closed. He spoke slowly, tonelessly, as if he were falling asleep. "You have a bike?" he said.

"What, a motorcycle? Hell, no."

"You like bikes?"

"Sure. I like bikes. I don't know about that one, though," the boy said, pointing to the motorcycle on the platform. It had purple and orange flames painted on it, and was weighted down with a system of chrome pipes that gave it the look of being able to take off slantwise into the air like a rocket.

"You want to ride that one?" the man said.

"Hell, no."

"Sure you do. It's what you came for."

The boy laughed, not quite meeting the man's eyes. "How far do you think I'd get on it?" he said.

The man studied him for a minute, still with that sleepy

look about him; then he leaned forward, laid a finger lightly on the boy's wrist.

"Listen here," he said, "that ain't the one you want, anyway. This here's the one you want." He ran his hand over the back wheel of a motorcycle that was pulled up under the platform. This one, which was no particular color, not having much surface to take the paint, was small and plain looking. It was stripped down to the most essential parts. The boy recognized it as the one the man had ridden the day before.

"How about if I showed you how to ride this one?" said the man.

"Sure," the boy said.

"You want to ride with me in the show today?"

"I guess not," the boy said.

"You scared?"

"It's not anything I'd consider doing," said the boy. He was thinking about the crowd of people looking on.

"Listen here," said the man, "if I'm going to teach you how to ride this here cycle, which I will do directly, I think you owe me the favor to ride with me, just one time around, maybe."

The boy looked at the motorcycle, which was barely visible in the shadows under the platform.

"It's hardly anything to it," the man said.

"How about if I do some work for you instead?" the boy said.

The man stood up and took a package of cigarettes out of his pocket. He turned away and lit one with his hands cupped around the match-flame. He stood looking down at the boy, his eyes narrow against the smoke from the cigarette.

"I guess not," he said, and walked away.

The old man opened his eyes when he heard the angel speaking. He was certain that he hadn't been asleep. He'd only been deep into memory pictures of when he was a boy, rowing in his father's rowboat on the river.

The day had progressed into the evening. The setting sun, shining vaguely through a curtain of dust, bathed everything in a deep yellow light.

The angel hadn't moved, nor was there any change in her expression, but hovering in the air above her head was a three inch flame of blue fire.

"Timothy Sawyer, thou hast fallen upon the thorns of shame," the angel said.

The old man remained slack in his chair, all the power in him fluttering just beyond his grasp, like a bird in search of a branch.

"Wherefore comest thou into this darkness?" the angel said.

"Get down," the old man whispered.

"Knowest thou not how to be abased?"

"Get down, Harlot," the old man said.

"Knowest thou not how to suffer need?" the angel said.

"She-goat daughter of Satan," the old man bellowed, rising from his chair. He lifted his cane over his head and descended the steps with a picture before him of the angel shattered into a thousand fragments; but when he stepped outward onto the hard ground and took hold of her by the wings, the blue flame leapt from her and began to consume all the bushes with their roses, and even the air between them, so that the old man was driven back by the heat of this conflagration and fell to his knees and then onto his side and covered his face with his hands.

After a long while, during which time he was swallowed up by a vast, windy darkness, he perceived far away a tiny white window of light. This window approached him, growing quickly larger, and when it reached him and broke over him he was ushered into the casual spaces of his own yard, with a mild wind blowing over him, and the three willows swaying listlessly from their station by the well.

"Sweet Jesus son of Jehovah," he said softly. He got to his feet and walked as fast as possible towards the shed.

When he had brought the truck, with many starts and stops, as close to the garden as he could get it, he climbed down out of it and approached the angel stealthily where

111

she lay in the tall weeds. She had tumbled over onto her face, exposing to the sky, side by side, the two small soles of her feet. Gathering all his strength he took hold of her by the ankles and neck, expecting to be staggered by the effort, but she weighed hardly anything. He climbed up into the truck with her, rolled her roughly with a clattering of wings and knees and elbows the whole way down the truckbed. He wedged her tightly under the rear window by pounding on her hip with his heel.

He drove in under a wooden arch on which were painted, in blue and gold letters, the words: The Gates of Paradise. He emerged out of the darkness into a confusion of calliope tunes and colored lights whirling in every direction. People leapt out of his way, and he turned the wheel first this way and then that, crazed by the lights and the noise, uncertain now of why he had come, or even where he was, knowing only that somewhere there if he looked long enough he would find the boy. Soon the truck went into a high scream, then gave a great lurch and died. The people around him stood completely still, staring at him in astonishment. When they began to move again, he opened the door and climbed down.

He was confronted by a face the size of a house. From the mouth of the face, the tongue rolled out and lay in the dust of the ground. A thin man in dark green trousers and a bowler hat stood to one side of it waving scraps of paper wildly over his head, yelling at the crowd. When he saw the old man standing by the truck staring in his direction, he shouted at him, "You've come to the right place, in here's what you're looking for," from which the old man understood that inside the mouth with the tongue hanging out of it he would find the boy. The man waved frantically at him as if the boy would be there only a few seconds longer. The old man got into a line of men that were walking directly up the tongue, and when he was even with the man in the bowler hat, the man struck him on the shoulder and said,

"Keep your hands out of your pockets, young feller, senior citizens is free."

As he moved through the mouth, the broad bodies of the men pressed in on him from all sides, holding him captive in the line and blocking from sight all that lay ahead. After a while he was pushed sideways by the current, and caught a glimpse of a small pink dog without any hair on it staring up at him out of a glass box. Then he saw a brown bull, larger than any bull he had ever seen, standing knee-deep in straw with his head down. A moment before the crowd closed in again, bearing him away, he saw on the bull a second, smaller, head, with a string of froth coming down out of a little calf-like mouth and only one eye gazing sadly outward in no particular direction. After that he was borne through a doorway into a dark room. There, in the darkness, everyone came to a standstill, finally. No one spoke, but the breathing in the room was heavy, and soon the heavy heat rolling in waves from the bodies of the men began to instill in the old man a condition of floating and forgetfulness. Out of the darkness an image welled up at him of the boy standing in a hallway with brown roses on the wallpaper. The boy looked at him blankly, then turned and disappeared into the shadows. This image came upon the old man with lightning speed, blowing over him like a cold wind, and invading him with the fear of being left alone. He began to shove forward toward a cone-shaped light that shone down on something taking place on a raised level. When he reached the front of the room, he saw a group of men above him looking down into a coffin. The men near him began to laugh when they saw he had pushed forward, and a number of them took him by the elbows and lifted him up on the raised level. "Step right up there, young feller, you ain't never too old," one of them said. The men beside the coffin stepped back and someone shoved him forward and he found himself looking through a glass lid at a woman lying in a casket of red silk. A dozen swordblades, with the sword-handles protruding outside the coffin, crossed over and under her body, forcing her into a subtle contortion.

"Whore," the old man said. He perceived by the corners of her mouth that the woman heard him say this.

"Whore," he said again, louder, and when he felt the men take hold of him, he broke away from them and rushed forward and spit on the glass over the woman's face.

A moment later, without any memory at all of how he'd got there, he was lying on the ground with the breath gone out of him in a dark, windy passageway between two walls. He discovered, directly over him, a narrow strip of the night sky with its mantle of stars.

He lay on his back remembering a time when he had gotten lost as a child in the wooded hills. He had lain all night under the pines, buffeted by a great sound, like the center of a bell. Now there began to rain down on him again, from the wedge of stars over his head, the same chilling vibrant hollow booming, invading him as it had the other time with a terror of aloneness.

He rolled over onto his hands and knees and found himself looking into the face of an enormous liver-colored dog. This dog, which gave no clue whatever as to its feelings, was attached to the wall by a length of heavy chain. The old man remained in the same position, eye to eye with the dog, picking up in his nostrils the stink of the garbage and bones that lay all about them on the ground, until it came to him that whether he lived or was murdered by the dog, the only action open to him was to rise and look for a way out of the enclosure. He got to his feet, searching about for his cane, then realized he'd left it at the house.

He went through a door near at hand and closed it behind him, and when his eyes had adjusted to the darkness he saw that he was in a tunnel that had a river running through it. He had to lower himself into the cold water of this river, which rose to his waist, and move through the tunnel with the current. The dark water pulled at him energetically, dragging his boots along the bottom. Finally it toppled him over and began to drown him soundlessly, bearing him all

114

the while towards an unknown place. After a few moments of this he was struck on the head by something solid. He grabbed the thing with both hands and hauled himself, floundering and grim in the face, over the side of a boat. When his eyes cleared of the fetid water, he saw before him on the boat two children, a boy and a girl, lying on a painted bench with their limbs intertwined. The boat reached the end of the tunnel and emerged into the bright lights, and the old man staggered off it onto a plank porch. He stood watching the boat as it reentered the tunnel on the other side, bearing away the children, who were still staring at him with the same expression.

"Listen here, young feller," said a voice behind him, "I don't care if you swim it or ride it, you owe me a half dollar."

The old man turned and saw a man with a hump on his shoulder prodding at another boat with a long pole. The boat bumped slowly along the planks, then was caught by the current and carried away. The man wore a long mud-colored slicker. One side of his face was solidly scarred, as if from a blast of intense heat.

It came to the old man then what the matter was. He understood that he was either asleep or dead and had drifted off the worldly plane. He decided that it was entirely possible that the angel had killed him in the garden, that everything he'd witnessed since that time, including the man before him with the boats, would have to be looked at in a whole new light. He studied the man closely and perceived about him a certain blue transparency, as if he had water flowing through his veins instead of blood.

"You in charge here?" he said to the man.

"Course I'm in charge here," the man said. "I'm the boatman."

The old man considered this for a minute. "Where am I at?" he said.

The man stopped and looked at him with his pole raised in the air. "Where do you think you're at?" he said.

"You tell whoever's in charge I'll be leaving here in a few minutes," the old man said.

"You ain't going funny on me, air you?" said the man.

"Where's the boy?" the old man said.

"Cause I ain't equipped for it," the man said. He moved toward the old man with the pole extended and prodded him on the hip with it. "Git on down the steps," he said. "I was only being funny about the half dollar. Senior citizens is free."

The old man stumbled down the steps and stood in the dust of a broad path with a river of people flowing past him. He decided not to move forward, even if he had to lie down on the ground, but then he caught sight of the boy not far ahead of him entering a gate. Over the gate was a sign that spelled out in bright lights the words: The Walls of Death. The old man began to run, shoving the people in front of him aside, calling, "Hey there, Joe-Boy! Wait up there! Don't you hear me?" But the boy disappeared through a doorway in the side of a barrel-shaped building.

When the old man reached the gate, he discovered the boy's cat asleep under a platform. She was curled up with her paws tucked into her breast. He was gladdened by the sight of her and tried to pick her up, but she struggled free and climbed up into one corner of the sign with the bright lights, out of his reach. She crouched there, peering down at him with a ruffled, sleepy look. He hurried on through the metal gate after the boy, taking it partway off its hinges in the process, but was stopped at the door by a dark-skinned dwarf in a leather apron. The dwarf pointed him up a rampway that was built onto the side of the barrel-shaped building. "You can see from up there," he said.

"But I want the boy," the old man said.

"Well, you're in luck," the dwarf said. "We've got one today." He took the old man by the shirtsleeve and turned him away from the door.

When the old man was halfway up the ramp, he looked down and saw a scar-faced man in a white outfit settle into the seat of a motorcycle. The motorcycle had purple and orange flames and the words, The Screaming Devil, painted on the sides. The man started the motorcycle up with a roar that flattened the old man against the side of the building. In the same instant a siren inside the machine went off and rose to a high pitch. The old man went in terror up the ramp and joined a crowd of people that stood behind a circular rail looking down inside a wooden pit. A small elderly woman with an entire stuffed bird sewn spread-winged onto her hat looked up at him and said, solemnly, "This here's called the walls of death."

The siren began circling the building outside, increasing its note of hysteria and calling up in the old man his fear of the unseen thing that sometimes prowled outside his cabin.

"Keep a close watch on that door yonder," said the elderly woman, pointing down into the pit. Soon the motorcycle roared through the door and began circling the bottom of the pit at high speed. The rider had tied a long white scarf with silver stars on it around his neck, and the siren, trailing behind him in the wake of this scarf, filled the pit with a sense of imminent and terrible disaster. The man drove out suddenly through the same door, but came back in a few minutes, this time on a much smaller machine with the boy riding on it behind him.

The old man gripped the rail with both hands and bellowed, "What in thunder!" but the motorcycle roared up the wall of the pit, drowning him out, and began to circle faster and faster. With each revolution it climbed higher up the wall, until everyone had to lean back as it passed to keep from getting hit in the face by the rider's scarf. The boy was pressed flat against the rider with his arms around his chest and his head thrown back. When the old man saw the look on his face he felt a ghastly cold rise in him and a sense of unavoidable and prolonged sorrow.

"He has taken him!" he cried out, "He has taken him!" He reached down to grab onto the boy, but in that moment the motorcycle rider, seeing his intention, let fly a blow with his arm that caught the old man full in the face, knocking him backwards onto the floor with all the hope gone out of him.

The woman with the bird on her hat came and bent over him and prodded him in the ribs with her toe. "If you have got the brains of a fish worm it don't stand out much on you," she said.

He rose immediately, with everyone watching, and made his way unsteadily down the ramp and up to the truck, which was still parked outside where he had left it. He climbed into the back of it and took hold of the angel by her elbows with the idea in mind of hurling her over the side and ramming her at high speed with the front end of the truck; but when he tried to lift her he was staggered by the weight. He moved her an inch and then another with great effort, finally rolling her over with a crash into the center of the truckbed. A crowd was gathering, but he took no notice of it. He sank to his knees and laid his face against the angel's breast. Pitting all his strength against her, he gave a heave and then another, with the veins about to burst in his face. In this way, he budged her inch by inch towards the side. It seemed to him as if he'd passed an eternity doing this, when he saw the dwarf looking at him over the side of the truck with dark and fascinated eyes. "He wrestles with the angel," the dwarf said in a low voice.

"He's wrestling with the angel," a woman said. Someone laughed. "He's wrestling with the angel," several others said, catching it up as if it were a tune they were starting to sing. Soon they were calling out, "Methusela" and "Old Man Moses," and coins sailed out of the crowd and rolled around inside the truckbed. A lead slug struck the old man on the face.

He was tilting the angel head first over the side when he heard the boy calling to him. He looked up and saw the boy coming, with the crowd falling back to let him pass, but when the boy was still some distance away, the dwarf gave a shout and pointed upward at the sign with the bright lights. There, transfixed against the colored lights and outlined by a shower of sparks, was the white-faced cat. They saw an explosion with smoke, the sign went dark, and the cat dropped to the ground like a stone.

In the silence that followed, the dwarf got down off the truck and crossed to where the cat lay in the dust, but as he bent to pick her up, the boy reached him and lifted him as if there was no weight in him, and clamped a hand like a vise around his throat.

When the boy took hold of the dwarf, the motorcycle rider moved out of the crowd and gathered up a long chain that lay under a platform nearby. He slung this chain with all his strength around the boy, and a heavy metal hook at the end of it landed up against the boy's head.

When the old man saw the boy fall, he got down out of the truck to go to him, but two men came out of the crowd and blocked his way. He felt the shock of a blow in his belly, and another between his eyes. He sank to the ground and had just begun to float off to one side in order to see everything more clearly, when the men took him under the arms and hauled him up into the cab of the truck.

"Git on the hell out of here," one of the men said. Then the old man heard a thump behind him, and he looked through the rear window and saw the boy lying in the truck-bed with one arm thrown over the angel.

He started up the truck and headed at high speed for the front gate. He scraped against one of the gate posts as he went through, but then he was out in the darkness with the colored lights growing smaller and smaller behind him, and no sound anywhere around him under the cloak of stars but the hum of the engine.

When he had traveled what he thought to be about five miles, he pulled the truck over to the side. He got out and made his way up a steep bank on his hands and knees and lay down on a grassy place at the top. It seemed to him as he lay there that the stars were descending on him like a net, but he rolled over and buried his face in the cool grass and held onto it with both hands.

The dawn had invaded the sky when he woke. The countryside hovered, shivering, under a pale, rose-colored light. He sat up and looked down into the road. He saw the boy lying stiffly in the same position in the truck, with his arm around the angel and his face against the hollow between her wings.

While the old man waited for the boy to move, a flock of birds not far off rose slowly in a spiral. They caught the first light of the sun like a shower of coins, then sank back and disappeared into the plowed field.

Unknown Feathers

He woke in the night in the room she had put him in when they found out he was not going to get well. He saw a pool of moonlight in one corner, and the long gauze curtains flapping out the open window like ghosts waving. He knew from the color of the shadows that it was near the morning. He looked past the foot of the bed and saw that the door was open into the hall, and that the top part of the stairs was caught in a square of moonlight crossed with thin black bars. Into this moonlight appeared his wife, coming barefooted up the stairs in her cotton slip. The black bars glided over her face and breast, and then she was in the room, standing in front of his chifforobe, which had the door hanging open and all the drawers pulled out. He watched her take his shirts down, with the hangers still in them, and all his trousers, and the brass ring holding his neckties. She took down also his two suits, the lightweight gray one and the brown wool one, which had hung there, unworn, for over twenty years. She held these clothes against her, lifting them high to keep them from dragging, and went to the top of the stairs. There she paused, then descended sideways, looking carefully to see where to put her feet.

He drew himself up on his elbow and gazed about the room. It looked bare and strange. His fiddle was missing from the oak bench beside his bed. Gone, as well, were all his catalogs, and the bell that she had given him to summon her. He reached out and felt along the window sill for his pipe and scraper, but they were gone, too. He lay back and stared at the ceiling, studying a watermark there, shaped like a crab, with which, over the past two months, he had grown very familiar.

After a few moments, his wife returned. This time she brought with her an old slat basket into which she gathered all his unwashed clothes that he'd thrown in a heap on the chair, and the belongings he'd collected on the shelf over the washstand, including his many bottles of medicine.

"What have you done with my fiddle?" he asked her. "And my catalogs?"

She turned and stared at him, then came and stood beside him. "I've reached the end of it," she said. "You have got to call the county people to come get you. I can't keep you any more." She pulled his blanket back until she had uncovered the small dog, which had curled itself into a ball against his leg. The dog raised its head sleepily and looked around the room. She lifted it by the skin of its neck and put it into the basket under the clothes. Then she went down the stairs. He got out of the bed and followed her.

Twice he had to rest on the stairs, braced against the wall until his head cleared. When he reached the landing at the bottom, he caught sight of himself in the old silver-spotted mirror which had hung there since he was a young man, newly married. He hardly recognized himself. He looked much older than his fifty years, and his eyes were large and dark and sunk into his head. He drew back from the specter of this, startled, as though from the face of an animal. Then he forced himself to look again, steadily, and this time was content that he'd kept himself shaven and clean. He was glad that he had been careful with his large moustache, which had remained glossy and reddish and full of vigor.

He had not been downstairs in many weeks, and everything looked smaller there, crowded, and not as clean as he remembered it. When he entered the kitchen, he found his wife waiting for him by the back door, holding the dog against her breast. She lifted the latch and went out, and then stood on the steps, keeping the screen door open for him. He came down beside her on the steps and took the dog out of her hands.

"The keys are in the truck," she said. "It's took too long and I can't take no more of it," she said. "Death happening for so long. Sleeping it. Eating it. Breathing it." She went back up into the house and closed both the screen door and the wooden door. He heard her throw the bolt.

He turned on the steps and regarded the horizon, which was a diffuse, silver-colored haze bearing in its center the white edge of the sun. Nearby, in the dark yard, he saw the bed they had always used for sleeping in the open on warm nights. Spreading over it, just as he remembered, was the big pear tree. This tree was caught in the first light, and crowded to the tip of every branch with buds.

Two weeks later, at around the same hour, he lay asleep under the flowering tree in the old iron bed. He lay exposed, in his suit of sweat-stained underwear, his long legs tangled in a brown blanket. He had grown a coarse beard, and his hair looked as stiff and unruly as a horse brush. His pale, sorrowing face was troubled by some dream that was bothering him.

The night had ceased its deep sounding and turned toward the morning. With the coming of the light, the full moon, setting in the northern quarter, had grown as thin and insignificant as a piece of old cheescloth.

In the countryside, the animals slept on. The coyotes were flung out on mounds of husks under the cactus. The old boar javelinas, fallen like stones in the open, ground their tusks. The little armadillos slept curled around roots underground.

In the henhouse, the hens quaked and teetered in deep sleep behind the dusty panes; the calf slept in the barn, next to the cow, who slept tied to the wall; and the two mares, sisters, slept with their faces touching. Even the metal-blue milk pails slept in a row, dreaming, in a slant of shadow by the bin of oats.

The man slept on his side, his hands pressed together between his thighs. All night he had been calling to his wife for water, and she hadn't brought it. Now he slept heavily in a stupor of thirst and exhaustion. Against his chest slept the small, hairless dog, which was about the size of a teapot.

Suddenly the back door of the house was flung open, and his wife rushed barefoot down the steps, carrying an iron pot full of water. She was a small, middle-aged woman with wiry arms and cropped hair the color of gunpowder. She wore a long-tailed khaki skirt, which flapped around her like a brown bird taking flight.

She ran full-speed across the yard, clutching the pot, and when she reached the man in his bed, she drenched him with the water.

He sat up, gasping, his arms held away from his sides, and the small dog leapt to the ground and began running in a circle, carrying on pitifully, as if it had been struck by lightning.

The woman held the pot upside down and shook out the last drops. Then she crossed the yard and went back into the house.

The man got out of bed and picked up the dog and scraped the water off it, holding it under the armpits. It continued to cry piercingly, the way an animal cries when it is certain that it has been killed. He shook it, then hugged it to him, then put his hand over its face, but nothing would console it. Finally he dropped it to the ground and stood at the foot of the bed, shaking.

"Mrs. Hart," he shouted at the house. "Mrs. Hart, I say. Can you hear me?"

There was no answer.

"I am leaving here today, Mrs. Hart. I am going to call the county people to come get me. Can you hear me?" The large white face of a horse, with dark eyes, appeared in a window of the barn.

"But first off you can expect a caller. For I aim to come calling on you, Mrs. Hart. I aim to enter the house today. And the county people can enter with me as witness."

The man put his hand on the bed railing to steady himself.

"What have you done with my fiddle?" he shouted. "And my catalogs?"

Again, there was no answer, only his own voice coming back at him from out of the rangeland.

124

"I will not be held accountable for what happens now! Not after you violated my personal belongings! Do you hear me?"

"Hear me? Hear me?" came the echo from the countryside.

"That, Ma'am, is where you went too far!"

"Too far. Too far."

He sat on the foot of the bed, hugging himself, shivering. "No food this whole time," he said.

He studied the small dog, which lay on its side, whimpering, glassy-eyed, as if it had lost all sense of this world.

"Soon's she hears a man's about to croak, she gets possessed to see if she can murder him."

He ran his hands roughly through his hair, shedding a shower of drops.

"Goes overboard with it."

He moved backward onto the bed and lay down, drawing his legs up. He lay with his back to the house, staring at the countryside. Every few seconds, a bout of violent shivering racked him. Beside him, on the hard ground, the small dog grew quiet and drifted into a stupor.

In the barn window, the mare moved over to make room for her sister. The two of them lifted their chins over the sill, and watched the man with deep interest, as if something new and unusual was about to happen to him.

Woody Hart woke to the sound of his wife taking an ax to a leg of his bed. He lay rigid, feeling a thud hit the bed every few seconds, aware that this had been going on for quite some time. He rolled over with an arm up, expecting to see the ax raised, but no one was there. He eased over to the edge and peered down and there was the small dog lying in the dust, looking stunned. After a second, the dog came alive and sat up, measuring the distance up onto the bed with a keen eye. Then it hove back on its haunches and shot through the air like a slung stone. It hit the side of the bed hard, and fell back into the dust.

"Fool dog has drove out his brains thataway long as I can recall," Woody said. "Doesn't never seem to learn."

He stretched out his hand to the dog, and it got to its feet, shaking, and began to prance about weakly. It came to him and sniffed the length of each of his fingers, then climbed into his palm, lifting its feet in carefully one at a time.

Woody put the dog inside his shirt next to his ribs and lay back. He looked through the branches of the pear tree and felt himself being drawn upward through the clusters of blossoms into the sky, which had flung itself over the earth like a bolt of blue cloth. He heard, far away, the calling of geese. "What month is this?" he said, listening to the geese coming, and soon they were close overhead, descending swiftly. He counted them as they went by, five geese, of an unknown feather, all faintly dappled and brown, like rooks.

"Headed for the sink hole, likely," he said.

He watched the geese drift down into the mesquites near the bend in the road. He pictured them settling into the crater of water, scummy and green, in its beach of pocked mud.

"Is it the month of geese?" he said. "By damn, what geese are those?"

He heard the door up at the house open and close, and he turned and called out through the bars of his bed, "Mrs. Hart, are you aware that the summertime is over, and it's into the time now of the migration of the birds?"

He watched his wife go into the shed and come out with a harness, and he called out, "It's getting on too late in the *year* to be turning the sod." She paid no attention to him. She went on into the barn. After a few minutes, she came out, leading the mule. The mule plodded in his harness, the loose straps trailing behind him.

"You take that animal out in the heat of the day," Woody said, "and come evening you'll be towing him home by the hind feet."

His wife drew the mule up in front of the shed and harnessed him to the plow and crossed with him between the trough and the windmill.

"Is it or is it not the fall of the year?" Woody Hart shouted.

But she was gone. He knew that she was headed around the shed, and would urge the mule into the wide plot bordered on three sides by prickly pear so dense that it was like a sea of turtles. He pictured the mule throwing his weight forward against the collar, and saw the woman's small sinewy arms, brown as saddle leather, steadying the blade in the cut.

A memory came to him then of his wife, maybe three, maybe four years ago, bringing his fiddle to him over a field of busted sod. He was mending fence. He looked up and saw her coming towards him over the rough furrows. He remembered how she had looked in her cotton dress, her feet bare, the fiddle held high in one hand and the bow held high in the other, and he said, "I recollect now why she brought that fiddle *out* there." He laughed a low laugh, and the small dog, roused up by this, shuffled against him.

"She never was up to no good, that one," Woody said.

He recalled, as if it were only the day before, the deep light of that evening and the shadow of the fence stretching further and further over the field. He remembered lifting the fiddle to his chest and drawing whispers out of it as she undid her buttons and slipped out of her garments, one by one.

Afterwards, she had gone back across the field alone, bare and sleek as a child who's been playing in the river.

"Wished I had that fiddle now," he said. "Maybe she'd feed me."

He reached inside his shirt and put his hand over the small dog. With its globular belly and thin feet, it felt like a warm, dry frog. He traced, with his fingers, the pea-sized cowlick on its breast.

"Wished I had that fiddle now," he said.

He dozed, and woke, and dozed again.

He dreamed that it was night, and he was standing in the middle of the yard in the moonlight, and he looked up and saw his fiddle, with the bow beside it, lying on the roof of the house. In that moment, he caught sight of his wife standing at the window, wrapped all around with the long gauze curtains. He raised both fists and shouted to her that he was coming in, that it was no earthly use to bolt the door, but before he had taken very many steps forward, the house broke into flame at all of its seams, like something made out of paper, and sank by slow degree towards the ground.

He woke, trembling and weak, blinded by the sun which blazed at him through the branches. He turned onto his side and studied the house. The tarpaper roof, littered with broken shingles, was set upon in that moment by sparrows falling on it like a shower of leaves.

Then he caught sight of something which interested him.

It was a length of fishwire, wrapped around a branch over his head, hanging down maybe two or three feet with a cork on the end of it.

He took the dog out of his shirt and set it in a twist of the blanket. Then he eased up, took hold of the wire and hauled it free. When he did this the limb snapped back, showering him with petals, and making him feel dizzy and frail. After a moment he crawled to the head of the bed and tied the fishwire tautly between two bars of the railing. He strummed on it, and it gave out a good sound that was a little like an acorn dropping down inside an old piano. He plucked on the wire rhythmically, pressing it up against the rail in different locations with his thumb, and this made a sound like eaveswater dripping into a barrel.

"Dogged if it ain't a regular sound," he said.

He played on, searching out the notes, until soon he was into some of his old tunes. He lost track of the time, propped against the head of the bed, making his music, singing with an increasingly full heart. The small dog crept up by slow degrees, and turned itself around deftly on his belly, and slept.

After a while, Woody became aware of someone on the road down near the sink hole. He looked over and saw a group of women approaching. He counted five of them.

He thought at first they were gypsies, but when they got closer he decided they must be the nuns from the old people's home in Twin Rivers, coming around on their yearly drive for bottles and rags. They were dressed in brown habits with the hoods thrown back, and seemed very relaxed and happy, looking about them as if vastly pleased to be out in this great wilderness of cactus and thorny mesquite.

As they passed through the gate, he saw that one of them had a light-haired child by the hand, a slightly built boy, not yet of school age.

They filed into the yard, smiling and waving to him, and the lead nun called out, "That was very fine music, Mr. Hart," and the others nodded and said, "Yes, indeed," and "Truly." They all came on towards him, looking tired and happy, as if they had reached the end of a long journey. They walked barefoot through the dust of the track, and when they were closer he saw that they wore, under their coarse habits, garments of fine white cloth which flashed at their wrists and ankles as they walked.

As they approached, he was overcome by shame regarding his state of attire.

"Mrs. Hart is in the sorghum field out back of the shed," he said, trying, with this information, to fend them off before they got any nearer, but they came on towards him.

"My, what a fine place to lie you have there, Mr. Hart," the lead nun said. "Do you mind if we rest here with you for a space of time?"

She had come right up to his bed by then, and she upended his bucket—which, to his profound relief, was empty at that moment—and settled herself on it, and then they had all arrived. They milled around him, making him feel dizzy and frail. They moved in and out of his line of vision, speaking in low voices, and it was something to do with an air they had, slightly, of taking charge of him, that afforded him a small sense of relief. He felt like an ailing turtle overtaken by a school of energetic fish.

Two of the nuns went behind him at the head of the bed.

129

Another crossed over to the base of the tree and pulled herself onto one of the lower limbs.

"I wouldn't put no weight on them branches," Woody said, but the nun rolled her sleeves to the elbow and climbed from one limb to another until she had reached a place high up. As she settled herself there, she was struck and lit up by the sun, and Woody looked closely, shielding his eyes with his hand, and saw that the light-haired child had made his way up there too, and was sitting on the branch beside her. The boy looked down through the branches, swinging his feet, and the sight of him sitting there, rocking back and forth with a pleased look, reminded Woody that two years ago there was a deck of planks with a roof over it in that very place in the tree. He hadn't thought about that deck in a long while. He remembered putting it together out of the boards and tin lining of an old trough which had leaked so badly that no amount of repair could make it right.

Thinking back on this deck in the tree, he felt the chills from earlier that morning creep in on him again. He drew up his blanket and turned onto his side.

Beside the bed, the lead nun spoke to one of the others in a low voice and all the sounds—the voices of the women, the wind in the leaves, the heavy tread nearby of the two mares moving in the stall—began to drone, as if everything was happening in a huge, windy chamber.

Woody drew the blanket closer around him and looked far out into the countryside. There he saw a tired orange light approaching under a haze of dust which had lifted and covered the sun.

He remembered how strange that deck of planks had looked, like something that had fallen down into the tree from another planet.

"Sawed off the limb, by damn, and brought it down," he said.

He reached out his hand to the two nuns beside the bed. "Some years back there was a child on the way," he said, "and I put a deck up for it. I put a deck up in the tree for it to play in. But it was born dead."

He lay back on his pillow, watching the branch split the last inch, after the sawing, watching the deck descend swiftly, all of a piece, with an explosion of leaves and branches, on the ground.

He studied the deep orange light that was moving swiftly towards him across the cedars. It slipped heavily over him, and lit up the yard, and the slow blades on the windmill, and the roof of the house – like a wing on a long journey. The dust, which had come up heavily out of the rangeland, was filtering like smoke over the sun, and all he could think of was the sight of that branch falling, and falling, and his wife weeping – a high, weak sound with no heart left in it. It made him tired to hear it.

On that day, two years ago, the dust had defeated him. He'd been out in the eastern sector that whole morning, shearing, and by noon was full of wool grease and thorns. He was working with his friend, John, who had his sheep there, too, and the three hands from town that they were hiring by the day. They'd gone through no more than half the bunch they'd brought in, but the dust had begun to blow and it was the middle of that kind of white-heat draught that can drive a man to the staggers and raise up for him, in the faraway stretches, whole cities of celestial light – and so at midday they turned out into the pens the ones that were left and put the rest of it off into the cool of the following morning.

By the time he arrived home, the dust was a wall around him, out of which the thorn trees and the outbuildings loomed suddenly and came towards him like shapes in a dream. In the barn, his horse pulled out of the loosened saddle and whirled in the stall, squealing with raw temper, maddened by the dust which drifted through every crack and could not be gotten away from.

He wrapped his head in his jacket and felt his way along the paddock fence through the dervish sand, and when he had climbed the steps and pulled open the back door against the wind and latched it behind him, the house was deeply and strangely quiet. He recalled that his wife had gone out on foot early that morning to look for a lamb of hers, a dark one that she'd been raising, that had gotten out of the barn. The worry came over him that she'd gotten lost herself. He called to her, and looked around the kitchen for some sign of her, but could not tell, even, what was laid out on the table, for the room was filling with dust and had grown very dark in the last hour. He went to the pump and tried for a long time to draw water, though there was hardly a cupful left in the bucket to prime with. Finally he pulled open his shirt and went up the stairs to the basin in the bedroom. The small portion of water there was laid over thickly with dust, but he cupped it in his hands, and raised it to his face. Then he heard, downstairs, a single muffled cry which he knew, without need for any questioning, was his wife gone into labor with the child.

He descended the stairs two at a time and found her lying on her side on the bare mattress in the spare room. She was holding onto the bedrailing, and her face was streaked with dust and tears. She had thrown the covers onto the floor, and nearby was the cradle laid over with a long gauze cloth. The air in the room was very deep with the dust.

He slipped his hands under her, thinking to carry her directly to the truck, but she rolled away and began to breathe rapidly, with a little cry for each breath. Then she drew a long shuddering breath, and held it, and in the deep silence before she breathed again, he watched a stain bloom and spread swiftly on the mattress under her.

"It's now! It's now!" she said, drawing breath rapidly, and then the deep breaths came again, and then the silence. This time she gripped his sleeve in one hand, staring at him with eyes that could not see, and lifted up slowly with the strain.

He unfastened her trousers and hauled them off her and rolled her over, and she let out her breath in a long high wail.

Her legs looked very small and white, and now he could spread them open and crawl up and kneel between them, and this time when she fell silent and bore down, he looked

132

and saw the bulge of the child's head, a taut oval spreading wider, and inside the oval a patch of blue scalp with hair.

"Push, push," he said. "Yes! Push!" but she let go of the air, and lay back, gasping, and the child's head was drawn back up into her body.

He reached past her legs and took hold of both her hands. "It's going to come right now, oh, now," she said, drawing the deep breath. "Yes, it's coming now," he said. "It's coming. Push. Push," he said, bearing down with her, and this time, in the long silence, it was as if they were rocking together in a small craft, and holding onto her was like pulling on the oars. Then the oval bloomed over the head once more, and the image came to him of the sheep getting turned out of the wool, one after the other—of the wool mat laying back first at the neck, then off the shoulders, then lifting away from the flanks, and the sheep emerging white and clean and without blemish, as though getting born into a new life. His wife shuddered violently and called out, "I'm falling. Oh, Woody don't let go of me," and all this while the child was sliding out slowly, with great dignity.

It was blue as a hyacinth, folded, glistening. It was smooth as if it were made out of marble. It lay quivering on the bed, already filming with the dust.

"Don't let go of me," his wife said.

"It's got to breathe," he said.

"I'm falling, Woody, don't let go!"

"It's got to cry," he said, and he took the child up by the feet and shook it, but it didn't cry.

"Is it the child?" she said.

"Jesus, God," he said. "You can't help me." And he laid the child face down and knelt over it and pressed on it heavily to make it suck air; but though he worked at this tirelessly—forgetting his wife, and the dust, and the house shuddering in the hot wind, and the vast tracts of land upon which, by now, most of his sheep lay dying in the heat— though he kneaded and pulled on the small body, the child remained still. Finally he stopped. His wife had raised herself up on her elbow, and was watching, and she reached out to touch the child, but he pushed her hand away, and brought out his knife, and severed the cord.

"The child is dead," he said.

"No, listen," she said, holding onto his arm, "I want to have it."

"The child is dead," he said.

He pulled the long cloth off the cradle, and wound the child up in it tightly, solid and white. He took this bundle out of the room and laid it on the dough-board in the kitchen. Then he backed off, and stood in the doorway, watching. The white cloth was soon laid over by a fine powdering of dust, like flour.

He was brought out of his reverie by the sound of the plow dragging, and he looked back through the bars of the bed and saw his wife coming in from the field. She halted the mule in front of the shed and leaned on his shoulder. She had a handkerchief knotted around her head, against the sweat, and was all over one color from the dust. The mule stood with his head down, the plow still bound to him by the harness.

"Couple of jack-straws," Woody said. "Either one moves, the other'll drop."

His wife unstrapped the plow, and led the mule into the barn.

After that the light began to deepen and evening came on slowly. Woody wondered what had happened to the day. Over his head, the tree began to shimmer, and he looked up and saw that the nun and the child had decked every branch, even the small twigs, with crystal glass. It had become very quiet, and the wind, which was dying down, stirred the tree and beat the pieces of glass against each other like chimes. Gradually the sun descended into deepening layers of color out over the farthest reaches of the cedars, and Woody lay still on his pillow, listening to the chimes and watching the shadow of his bed lengthening into the yard like a giant crab.

134

When he spoke, it felt as if the words came from him like a river moving slowly.

"Why has she brought me no water?" he said.

"Did you call to her for water?" someone said, and he turned and saw the lead nun standing beside him. Her voice had the sound of someone calling up out of a well.

"Yes, I called for water. I called for water plenty!"

"Well, she finally brought it to you, didn't she?" she said.

By then he could hear other voices. He saw light flickering, like the noon sun through the foliage, and then the nuns were leaning close over him and he felt a great wind blowing past as if they had pulled his bed into a tunnel, and then he slept.

He woke, and it was night. The full moon, crossed with short rags of clouds, cast a light over the countryside, that was like a white sea with the waves halted.

Something moved nearby, and he looked closely into the shadow of the tree and saw his wife standing there, wrapped in a blanket. She gazed at him with eyes full of dark feeling. He moved over to make a place for her in the bed, and her blanket opened like a husk, and she came out of it bare and frail in the moonlight. Her little white breasts looked childish and exposed, and her limbs reminded him, as they always had, of those of a half-grown boy. She came in beside him, slipping one leg under him, and crossing the other over him, and eased herself close up into the hollow under his arm.

Then they lay still, taking in the night sounds. He heard the frogs lamenting by the sink hole, and the crickets' wall of song, and, raining steadily down on everything, the massive hollow booming of the stars.

He watched, over their heads, the tree sailing through the night sky swiftly, with strong purpose. It bore the full moon with it, netted in its branches like a chalice, or a giant moth.

He lost track of the number of days he'd been without

water. He began to see visions of it shimmering in the air above him. The shade from the tree was scant in the buffeting white waves of heat. He lay in his bed under the noon sun, wondering what it would be like to have a thunderstorm roll up overhead and drench him, and sometimes it felt to him, indeed, as if water of some kind were very close; but then he would hear the dog whine, and feel it licking the salt-sweat from his hand, and he would recall that they were now into some dry portion of the summer, and that there would be many days still ahead without rain.

He picked up the dog and set it on the ground beside the bed, hoping maybe it would relieve itself and then go and find water, but it only stood weakly, looking down at its own shadow lying between its four feet like a little puddle.

"Go on over and sit up on the step there, buddy," Woody said. "Maybe she'll take notice of you."

He thought he heard the sound of the pump handle then, and he looked over at the house and was surprised to see that the five nuns had come calling on them again. They were approaching in a group.

"Don't take one more step in my direction without bringing water," he called out, and the lead nun raised her hand and answered, "Indeed, Mr. Hart, that's exactly what we had on our minds. We were thinking maybe you'd like to go down with us to the river."

He laughed at this, thinking of the blistered land with its few sink holes of water. "What river is that?" he asked, and she said, "The one we passed on our way here."

Then they were surrounding him on all sides and lifting him easily until he was on his feet beside the bed.

"Now, hold on here," he said. "I believe this is something has got to be talked over first with Mrs. Hart," but they had slipped their arms around him by then, and the lead nun pointed down the road and said, "It's only just a short distance over the rise, Mr. Hart. Did you think it was in some faraway country?"

They moved with him slowly forward, and he wondered what rise she could be referring to, for the land was as flat as a griddle. He looked ahead and caught sight of the light-haired child standing at the gate, looking back and waiting.

"If we're going out into the pasturage," Woody said, "she'd want to know," but they bore him steadily on across the yard and through the gate, and when they passed over into the open country he looked ahead a short distance and saw the child standing in the dust of the road, motioning to them to come faster.

"I wouldn't let him wander far," Woody said, and then he felt the road lifting under them and they started slowly up a long grade. When they reached the top, he looked down at the river, vast and slow-moving, with the light on it almost too bright to be looked at, and now he remembered it well, with its little copse of willows, and its swaying grasses. He saw brightness strike and spread swiftly where the wind scuffed the water.

"It looks like a good place to lie down right there under them willow trees," he said.

They went through the tall grass slowly, with the child running ahead of them, leaving a wake of silver in the green.

"She should know to come here," Woody said. "Could one of you run tell her? She's probably still out in the field behind the shed."

They gathered close around him, then, in the shade under the willows. He felt himself being eased down, and he thought he saw the child going naked into the water. "Time to bathe him," the lead nun said, and he thought at first she meant the boy; but then they were bending nearer, and they had taken off their coarse brown robes. As the water rose around them, the rays striking off them blazed brighter and brighter, until all he could see were their faces in the wide slow river of light.